CHANDRA

Her grandmother was anxious. 'Jaisalmer is a long-long way off. Away out in the desert. Nineteen hours by train. And then on to a farm twenty kilometres further yet. If anything goes wrong—'

Chandra was eleven and she was about to be married to a boy aged sixteen. She and her parents were very excited and took no notice of her grandmother. What could go wrong to spoil her happiness? Her father had chosen well for her, and they'd be very happy together, she was sure.

But out in the desert, she realized she was alone and far from home. She sat in the darkness of her little room, unwilling to accept what had happened to her. She sat day after day, night after night, in heat and cold, thirst and half-starvation, staring dully, praying, weeping, without an identity.

She tried to remember who she was, she hung on to her name. 'My name is Chandra. And I'll not let it be forgotten.'

Frances Mary Hendry was a teacher in Scotland for over twenty years. She has also run a small guest house which only had visitors in the summer, which meant she would write all winter. Until 1986, when she won the S. A. C. Literary Award for her book *Quest for Kelpie*, the only writing she had done was pantomimes for her local drama club—something she still enjoys doing. She also won the S. A. C. Literary Award for *Quest for a Maid* in 1988 and has had five other books published since then. *Chandra* is her first book for Oxford University Press.

Her other interests include history (until men started to wear trousers), gardening, embroidery, and amateur dramatics—especially pantomimes.

D0414884

CHANDRA

To Prasun and Chandra Basu, of Calcutta,
with thanks for their kindness and criticism,
hospitality and help.

Other books by Frances Mary Hendry

Quest for a Kelpie
Quest for a Maid
Quest for a Babe
Quest for a Queen – 1. The Lark
2. The Falcon
3. The Jackdaw
Jenny

CHANDRA

Frances Mary Hendry

Oxford University Press
Oxford New York Toronto

Oxford University Press, Walton Street, Oxford OX2 6DP

Oxford New York
Athens Auckland Bangkok Bombay
Calcutta Cape Town Dar es Salaam Delhi
Florence Hong Kong Istanbul Karachi
Kuala Lumpur Madras Madrid Melbourne
Mexico City Nairobi Paris Singapore
Taipei Tokyo Toronto

and associated companies in
Berlin Ibadan

Oxford is a trade mark of Oxford University Press

Copyright © Frances Mary Hendry 1995
First published 1995
Reprinted 1996

ISBN 0 19 271712 X

Cover photograph: R. A. Simpson Photographic Studios.

A CIP catalogue record for this book is available
from the British Library

Printed and bound in Great Britain by
Biddles Ltd, Guildford and King's Lynn

CHAPTER 1

Great News

'What's wrong with her?' Sangeeta's cheeky face was quite worried as she peered past the crowd. 'She usually bounces along, high-fly as a kite.'

Urvashi stood on tiptoe, her hand on her friend's shoulder to steady herself. None of the two thousand girls pouring into the Dr Manip Bhardwarsh School for Girls (English Medium) would be rude enough to jostle her, of course, but the pavement outside the school gate was uneven. She shaded her eyes against the brilliance of the morning sun. 'She's not limping.'

'She can't be worried about her marks. She's always tip-top, in everything except maths. Maybe she can't sleep in this heat. Mata puts bowls of ice round the beds, and we have the ceiling fans on all night, and I'm still too hot—I hate June, just before the rains! And you know Chandra's father is so poor, their house is like an oven. Could that be it?'

Urvashi shrugged. 'Am I Ganesha, to know all the secrets of the world? We'll soon find out, even at the rate she's walking.'

Chandra was pacing sedately along the lane towards the school, avoiding the potholes instead of jumping over them, ignoring the boy with the sugar-cane crusher where she often spent a few paise on a drink of the sweet juice, and the old man with newspaper bags of spiced noodles, which she loved. Calmly serene, she threaded her way among the swirling rickshaws delivering her fellow-pupils, and waded through the waist-high sea of five-year-olds tumbling happy and noisy out of the safe cages of the cycle school vans.

As she drew close, her friends relaxed. 'Ai, there's nothing wrong with her!' Urvashi said. 'Look at the smirk! Like a cat that's knocked over the cream jug! What's she playing at today?'

'Namaste!' Chandra didn't wave and call from a distance as usual; she touched her fingers together and murmured the greeting primly, with a polite, formal bow, as if to strangers. She looked like a model of the perfect pupil. Her sea-green uniform of cotton salwar trousers and kameez tunic down to her knees was even more spotless and crisply pressed than usual, her white dupatta scarf folded and pinned across her chest so that the ends fell gracefully behind her shoulders. The long black plait of her hair was tidily doubled up and held at the nape of her neck by a white bow. But her eyes were sparkling, not demure.

Her two best friends eyed her suspiciously. 'What's the joke? What have you been up to this time?' Urvashi demanded.

'Nothing! I promise, nothing! I've been a saint all weekend!' Chandra pretended to be hurt.

Sangeeta poked her ribs. 'Ha! You had to be good, with that catty-ratty old aunt of your father's staying with you. What have you done? Pushed her under a bus? Put salt in her tea?'

'Nahi—no! Nothing like that. But she . . . well—' She bit her lip to hide a grin, but couldn't stop herself snortling in suppressed glee.

'I knew it! I knew there was something!' Sangeeta squealed triumphantly. 'What's she done, then? Tell-talk!'

Giving up, Chandra grinned widely. 'Come inside, away from the rest!' She tugged her friends through the corrugated-iron gate, past the crush of little girls splashing and chattering round the water pump, over to the furthest corner of the brick-hard yard, where they could squat on their heels in the shade of the big neem tree in a close little trio, arms round each other's shoulders to steady themselves, and be reasonably private.

2

'Quick!' Urvashi urged her. 'Miss Kapoor will be out with the bell in a minute. What did your great-aunt do?'

'OK. I told you she was—'

Sangeeta, always in a hurry, interrupted her. 'The nosiest old lady you'd ever had staying with you, ji haa, we remember. So?'

'So.' Chandra's big dark eyes were full of glee. 'She kept scolding me for—oh, everything. Not washing Deepak's sports shorts white-bright for his basketball match on Saturday—why are boys so stinky? Or not rolling my bed-mat tidily, or making heavy louchis—'

'She couldn't say that!' Urvashi protested. 'Your baking's almost as good as my mother's!'

'Ai, how nice of you!' Chandra bowed thanks. 'But she was always complaining-criticizing. The guest is god, mata says, and it's a woman's duty to be obedient and good-tempered and respectful, and so I was, truly I was! Making polite, nani calls it.' They all giggled. 'Besides, I didn't want to let mata down. Bapa's family are all dreadfully traditional.'

'And so? Ai, hurry up!' Sangeeta was losing patience.

'And so, you know we always go on Sunday afternoons to visit mata's mother? Yesterday bapa stayed at home with great-aunt. When we got home from nani's house, they were sitting cross-legged on the bed side by side like maharajahs in council, and bapa said he had some news for me.'

'Well?' Her two friends, sensing that she was coming to the point at last, leaned forward eagerly till all three dark heads were almost touching.

'Great-aunt said I wasn't too bad.' She imitated the old lady's sharp tones. 'Long-tall, of course, and her nose and neck are short, and she's skinny-thinny. But her skin's wheaten. She works well enough in the house, and she doesn't argue. Quite good manners, and at least she's not ruining her reputation sitting next to boys in class like a shameless European! Ai-ai, what a waste of time and

3

money for a girl to learn geography-history, just to run her husband's home and rear his children!'

Chandra's friends nodded at the familiar comments. 'Old ladies are terrible!' Sangeeta giggled. Urvashi tutted at her impertinence.

'Wait and hear! Bapa interrupted her, and said that yes, I was more modern than he liked, but it was nani who was paying for my schooling—I never knew that, but I suppose the boys' fees take all bapa's money. And anyway, she'd said that a modern girl was what he was looking for.'

'He?' Sangeeta pounced on the word. 'Who?'

'And our horoscopes matched well, and—'

'Nahi! Never!' Urvashi was open-mouthed in awe. 'You mean—'

'Yes!' Chandra gripped their hands in triumph. 'She'd come to inspect me, to see if I'd be a suitable wife for her grandson! I'm to be married!'

'Oh, you lucky—May you have a hundred sons! How old is he? Is he handsome? Rich?' Sangeeta exclaimed all in a breath.

'Congratulations, of course, and blessings from all the gods, but how can you? It's illegal, you have to be eighteen to be married, and you're only eleven.' Urvashi was always correct.

'Oh, Vashi, who ever cares for that?' Sangeeta was bouncing on her heels. 'There's a dozen-hundred girls here married, Lakshmi was when she was six! She's going to her husband's family when she's finished Grade Ten. What are you going to do, Chandra? Tell us!'

Like her, Chandra could scarcely sit still. 'Well, I will, when I get a chance, chitter-chatter! You know what bapa's like. He says he wants me safely married before I start getting flighty like Western girls.'

Urvashi nodded approval, but Sangeeta clapped her hands, shaking her head side to side and sighing theatrically. 'Too late for me! I'm in love with Narander Singh.'

4

'I thought it was Sudhir Nair? Or my big brother Kirpal? But we're not all as sexy as sparrows! Ai!' Chandra fell over as Sangeeta poked her again. 'Ah, look at that! You jungly!' She brushed the dust from the knees of her salwar, and exchanged a few playful slaps with Sangeeta. 'Now sit quiet or I won't tell you! Bapa's been writing letters for weeks, but he only told mata last week, and said I wasn't to be told till I'd been inspected-approved. So now it's all arranged. His name is Roop, Roop Sharma. He's sixteen. His father is bapa's second cousin, Omparkash Sharma, with a big farm near Jaisalmer—'

'You're going to live on a farm? Ai-ai!' Urvashi's heavy eyebrows rose steeply in derision. 'You're even scared of the cows on the pavement! What'll you do on a farm?'

'Stay indoors, I expect!' Chandra grinned. 'They're very conservative in Rajasthan! But it's mostly goats there, bapa says, and camels, away out in the desert. I'll not be on the farm, anyway, except visiting. Roop's going to run a tourist hotel, so I'll stay here to finish my education while he does his training. By that time Kirpal will be married, and maybe Deepak as well, and their brides' dowries will help pay mine, as well as putting Kirpal through university. And bapa has insurance for it, too.' Her friends nodded seriously. Dowries were a dreadful expense for a girl's family.

'Are you going to meet before your wedding?' Sangeeta asked.

'Nahi, don't be silly! Mata's family might let me meet the boy, but not bapa's.' Chandra shrugged. 'But great-aunt let me see a photo of him. He's not handsome, but not ugly either. He looks cheerful, and he's modern-minded, great-aunt says, as if it was a fault! I'm sure we'll get on well.' She chuckled. 'Great-aunt took a photo of me away with her. Just to let him see what he's getting. If he's so modern, he might refuse me!' They all giggled at the incredible idea.

'I'll insist on meeting my husband,' Sangeeta declared firmly. 'My family are progressive!'

5

'Why bother? You wouldn't dare refuse him!' Urvashi snorted.

'Oh, yes, I would! If I didn't like him, I would so!'

Her friends just laughed at her. A girl to refuse to marry her parents' choice of a husband for her? Well, it did happen, but . . . 'You think this is Bombay, and you're a rich-bitch film star? You want to marry for love, like a soppy-silly westerner!' Chandra made a jeering face.

As Sangeeta stuck her tongue out at her, Urvashi returned to the main point. 'When's the wedding? Are we invited?'

'Of course! It's in a fortnight.'

'You'll never be ready in time!' Sangeeta wailed.

Chandra shrugged. 'It's the best time for us for nearly a year, the astrologers say, and bapa doesn't want to wait. June twentieth, at one o'clock. Roop's taking a few days off school—ai, there's Miss Kapoor coming! With our mark-sheets! Come on! We can talk about it at dinner-time.' Chandra scrambled to her feet. Hand in hand, the three girls ran to line up with the other girls of their class for the morning pooja.

'We give blessings and prayers to you, Saraswati!' Bowing to the image of the goddess of learning above the classroom door, Miss Kapoor frowned. Faint whispers were spreading through the lines, instead of the reverent hush she was used to. 'Give us the seriousness to study hard, and help us to remember what we are learning today.' The thrilled whispers grew. 'Dr Manip Bhardwarsh, we bless your memory. Please to turn our minds from all foolish distractions, inspire us to work and learn well, not to be frivolous or silly!' Under her glare, the murmurs faded. 'Help us learn to think for ourselves, be good women, inspire our families, our husbands, our children, to build up our country into a glorious society of freedom and justice for all.'

The short, stout little lady nodded in satisfaction at the respectful silence, and stood aside to let the girls file in quietly. She had settled them down. It was something to do with Chandra, she felt; well, she'd find out soon enough.

While the sixty-eight girls packed on to the bench seats in groups of four at each long, narrow table, the teacher stood at her desk as usual, her cream and orange sari and toning orange blouse bright against the grey cement walls in the squares of light from the barred windows. 'Good morning, girls.' She bowed politely.

They rose to bow to her, touching their palms together in respect. 'Good morning, Miss Kapoor.'

After a few seconds, when they were all sitting again, she held up a sheaf of papers. 'As you can see, girls, I have your exam marks here.' There was a quick rustle of excitement. 'Yes. And this is the great day for this class. You have all done very, very well. Your total marks are best in the whole school. Your names will be in the Year Book as the winners of Grade Seven this year!' They all clapped in pride and delight. She held up a finger to stop them. 'And also, I have a pleasure to announce that one of you has done exceptionally well indeed—has topped in no less than three subjects, over all the girls of your grade. Chandra Sharma, will you stand up?'

In her seat right at the back corner, Chandra slipped out into the passage and stood up proudly.

'Chandra, the mathematics was your poorest subject, you only got 79%. But in the geography, you topped with 87%. In the Hindi you came second—' at the class's groan of dismay, she smiled '—by one mark only, with 86%. You topped in the history, with 92%, and in the English with no less than 93%! And you have won a very good place among the top six in the dance, and in art, in homecraft and in music. You are top in the whole year, in the total marks! Well done!'

The whole class clapped and cheered. What a marvellous day for Chandra!

Miss Kapoor wondered why they were so enthusiastic. It was good to have a classmate win the first place, and she

7

knew Chandra was popular, but surely this was a bit too much! There was definitely something going on!

Blushing, biting her lip in proud bashfulness, Chandra felt she was ready to explode like a firework. Top in the whole year! And English would be useful, to a hotel owner's wife. Accha! No, not 'accha'; very good!

CHAPTER 2

Preparations

Chandra and her mother wrote letters, and visited all the family who lived near enough, to invite them to the wedding. They all promised gifts—dishes, a tin box for clothes, chairs, a clock, cups, mats, a quilt, cutlery. The presents from mata's family, of course, were better, because they were richer; and it was one of them who was the only person who seemed less than delighted.

Chandra's mother's mother was well-off, real middle-class. She lived with her son Raj, his wife Amrita and their four sons in a big flat away on the far side of Delhi, not far from the rich colonies where the foreign diplomats lived. When mata told her the great news, nani immediately clapped her hands. 'Accha! Congratulations, granddaughter! May you and your husband have many sons and many years together!' But as the flood of smiles and questions, explanations and exclamations rushed on, the old lady's sweet face became more thoughtful. After a while she sent Chandra's mother, with Amrita and the boys, out to buy some sweets to celebrate, and as they left, she patted the settee by her side. Obediently, Chandra came to sit down. What was worrying nani?

'Chandra, my dear. Are you sure you're happy about this?'

'Happy? Ah, ji haa, nani!' Chandra nodded vigorously sideways.

Her grandmother tut-tutted doubtfully. 'Jaisalmer is a long-long way off. Away out in the desert, what, eighteen, nineteen hours by train, and longer by bus? And then you must go away on, to a farm about twenty kilometres further yet. If anything goes wrong—'

9

'Ai, nani, what will go wrong?' Chandra shook her head reassuringly. 'If my mother-in-law doesn't like me, I'll just try harder to please her. Don't worry. I'll be OK.'

Her grandmother sighed. 'I suppose so. You're a good girl, my dear. You do your best. But somehow... Your bapa's family are all so traditional . . . ' She paused, her soft lips pursed in thought, smoothing her sari with a thin, wrinkled hand. 'In the city here, we're modern. But even I wear a white widow's sari, and I'd not dream of remarrying. And out in the country, it's like a hundred years ago . . . But your parents must know best, of course, and if the young man is a cousin . . . ' She shook her head, with one of the impish smiles that Chandra loved. 'You know your mata married for love?'

'What?' Chandra gasped. 'Mata? And bapa? Like Europeans? Never!'

'Oh, don't ever tell your bapa!' her grandmother chuckled. 'She saw him in the library, and fell in love with him. I nearly did myself! He hasn't changed much; he's still handsome and elegant, almost military, with that thin moustache. He wasn't well off, but it wasn't his fault. You know the story?'

Chandra nodded. 'Bapa's father was taking the family home on their scooter from a visit to the temple when a bus hit them and didn't stop. Grandfather was badly crippled, and bapa's leg didn't heal straight. The farm had to be sold to pay the hospital fees. Bapa wanted to join the army, but with his bad leg . . . So he went into the bank.'

'Ji haa. He was low down, but he had good prospects, we thought a Rajput would get promoted fast. He was a good man, he looked after his parents till they died, and his caste was right, so we agreed.' Nani hummed thoughtfully. 'I wonder if we did the right thing. If we'd got to know him better—his own manner loses him chances, he's so stiff, so easily offended, and he likes beer too much—but I shouldn't be saying this to you.'

Chandra's lips twitched, but she felt uncomfortable. It wasn't beer, it was whisky when he could afford it, though she couldn't tell nani that, of course. Criticize her own father, even for something as shameful as drunkenness? It was bad enough to be listening to nani doing it.

Her grandmother patted her hand reassuringly. 'Anyway, we arranged it with his family as if they'd never met. He'd have been horrified if he knew.' She shook her finger at Chandra. 'And your "modern-minded" Roop will probably be just as traditional.' She chuckled at Chandra's expressive rolling eyes, and then sobered. 'What's your mother's name, my dear?'

Chandra stared. 'Name? Mata's name? Is it—it's Varahi. Isn't it?' She was frightened, somehow.

Her grandmother nodded. 'Her husband calls her "my wife", you and your brothers call her "mata", I call her "beti". In some places, she'd be called "mother of Kirpal", and nothing else. A woman's name can be lost, forgotten, among her relationships. Ji haa, her name is Varahi. She has a BA degree, did you know? And she was a librarian. But when she married, your father told her she must give it all up to look after him and their children, and she obeyed. Tradition says that it is the mother who creates the atmosphere in a home. She has created happiness.' She paused, an eyebrow raised. Chandra nodded; most of the time, it was true.

Nani nodded in satisfaction. 'Yes. She's been fairly happy herself, I think, because he is a good man, even if he is poorer than we thought he'd be, and . . . irritable.' Well, that was one way to put it. He didn't use his stick only for walking . . . Four welts on Chandra's legs ached in memory of the last time he'd been drunk, but she said nothing. It was his right, and daughters didn't complain about their fathers. 'Besides, she has had her family only an hour away, to talk to. But you'll be away out alone.'

Oh, this was silly! 'Ai, why should I be unhappy, nani? Roop's nice, great-aunt said so. And besides, it's a woman's duty to love her husband and serve him, to worship him as her god. Great-aunt used to pray to her husband every morning, she said.'

11

'That's your bapa's family.' Grandmother sighed. 'My own nani did so, also. But things are changing nowadays. I insisted you go to school; you must know women have rights as well as duties! We fought for them at Independence, my friends and I, and we thought we had won them. Gandhi-ji and Nehru-ji said it, too.' She shook herself, trying to dismiss her doubts. 'But you're quite right. There's no reason for all this doom-gloom! A happy marriage is the same as a happy life. It's made, my dear, it doesn't come ready-built. You must work at it. Just—' she nodded decisively '—just remember that you can always depend on me to help you. Whether it's a month's rest away from your sixth baby—if you have so little sense!—or just a present. Like this one.'

Stiffly, she levered herself to her feet, opened a drawer in the shining old mahogany sideboard, and took out a roll of black cloth, which she smoothed lovingly. 'These were my own nani's. When you were five years old, she said they were to be kept for you, because you were her image.'

Chandra smiled up at the old brownish photograph of her great-great-grandmother, posed stiffly beside her husband, the wreath of marigolds hung on the frame always fresh and bright. Yes, she'd often been told she looked like her. But what had nani kept for her?

Her grandmother untied the crimson cord and spread the silk on the table. The contents spilled red and gold like lava from a volcano; a magnificent set of jewellery, heavy and intricate.

'Ai, nani! Rubies! So beautiful! The goddess Lakshmi herself can't have finer!' Chandra was almost afraid to touch them.

Her grandmother laughed with pleasure at the girl's delight. 'Try them on!' She helped Chandra pin in the heavy ear-rings and slip the supporting loops round the top of her ears; fit in the two-inch-wide nose-ring, and its cheek-chain of tiny jingling gold flowers, that clipped into her hair; to fasten the matching triple chain of the boss on her forehead, and the deep spread of the necklace with its three pendants; to squeeze her small hands into the wide swirl of the bangles.

In front of the mirror, Chandra moved into the sunlight, hummed a tune and swayed so that red and gold gleams of reflected light danced all over the room. 'Ah, thank you, thank you, nani-ji!' She bent to touch her grandmother's feet in respect and gratitude. 'And you, great-great-grandmother-ji!' She bowed to the photograph, and reached up to touch it as well.

'Ah, I remember my nani wearing them at my own wedding.' Nani sighed at the memory. 'She was so beautiful, like a maharani . . . ' She sniffed hard, and returned to the present. 'Now remember, these are yours. Amrita always wanted them, but they've been kept specially for you. They are a wedding gift from my nani, to you. They're not part of your dowry. That belongs to your husband. But these are yours.'

Chandra nodded, hardly listening, still humming and dancing with delight at the gorgeous gift. She sobered suddenly. 'Nani, what's your name? And what was your grandmother's?'

The old lady's eyes brightened. 'That's the idea! My name is Mira, and my nani's was Deepshikha, grand-daughter.' Her eyebrows rose quizzically.

'Chandra.' Chandra grinned, understanding what her grandmother wasn't saying. 'My name is Chandra. And I'll not let it be forgotten.'

The next month flew past. Every day, Chandra and her mother lit the sacred lamp and made a special pooja at the little shrine on the windowsill, with the photo of great-grandfather and the tiny statuette of Shiva. They visited the local temple to pray for the success of the marriage, taking gifts of flowers, money, and perfume for the elephant-headed son of Shiva, Ganesha the remover of obstacles, god of good beginnings, of wealth and of marriage; and for Shiva's female half, his wife Durga, the mother goddess, specially from Chandra and her mother. The brahmins weren't impressed by the gifts bapa could afford. 'Priests!' bapa complained. 'Fat, greedy idlers!' But he'd never think of doing without the gods' blessings.

Mata and Chandra scrubbed the cement floors of their rooms and painted them holy orange, drove the boys to whitewash the walls fresh and bright, sprayed cockroach killer everywhere, borrowed bedspreads and dishes from all their family and friends. Chandra was used to mata's fussing, but felt she was filling the bowl to overflowing this time; every night she was tut-tutting, shaking her head, sighing, muttering, 'Fifty—sixty—where can they sit? Ai-ai . . . Who else has chairs I can borrow . . . ?'

At last, bapa snapped one night, 'Ah, you can stop that hint-hinting! I heard you the first time. I've hired the wedding room.'

This was what mata had been working for, but she pretended to argue. 'Ai, how generous! How noble! But are you sure? Is it worth so much expense? This is the finest flat in ten streets! Who else has two whole rooms, as well as a washroom and a kitchen, for just five people? And electric lights in all the rooms, even the washroom? And none of the stairs broken? And even a fridge!' Proudly her eyes caressed the only slightly chipped second-hand cream box in the corner of the living-room beyond the wide wooden bed.

In spite of his pleasure at the compliments, bapa snorted. 'Don't be foolish, wife! It's too pokey-holey for all these crowds we must entertain. I'll not be shamed before my family—or yours! The wedding room it must be. And then the feast, and gifts. Always more rupees—girls are truly a curse!' Even through her joy, Chandra felt guilty.

Eventually, as if reluctantly, mata bowed her head in agreement. 'Ji haa, your will is my law, of course.' She winked at Chandra behind his back. This was how to manage a husband; one way, at least!

There was, glory of glories, a sari to buy for the ceremony, the first Chandra had ever worn, in flame-red silk. Well, it looked like silk. When it was tucked round the waist of her petticoat over her new red blouse, the gold-trimmed end draped to the correct length over her head, and all the rest of the six yard length pleated into graceful folds and tucked in, Chandra gazed at her reflection in the long mirror in the shop. 'Ai, mata, this is . . . this is lovely! Thank you, bapa-ji!' She bowed to his feet in gratitude.

He grunted. 'It should be. But 400 rupees is far too much . . .'

While he bargained, mata drew Chandra off to one side to change back into her school uniform. 'Don't speak about a new sari for me, beti,' she warned her. 'I still have my own pink silk wedding sari. Besides, your bapa has lost another promotion.' Ah. That was why he'd been so irritable these last few days, Chandra thought. 'Just don't mention it at all, or his pride will be hurt that we need to save him money. He could even insist on buying me one, and we can't afford it, not really.' Mata sighed. 'Men can be so touchy!' She and Chandra exchanged superior women's smiles, and when bapa announced triumphantly that he'd got the price down to just 270 rupees—over a week's salary, Chandra thought, he was so generous to her!—they applauded his skill and forcefulness, and quietly said nothing about a sari for mata.

And at last the day came . . .

CHAPTER 3

The Wedding

On Chandra's wedding day they were all up well before dawn, boiling water in the kitchen to scour off the greasy dirt of Delhi even more meticulously than usual in the tiny washroom. Under the garlands of mango and basil leaves that bapa and the boys had strung up, bapa offered grandfather and Shiva scent and milk, fire, and sacred Ganges water. Then he and the boys went out to the barber's to be ceremonially shaved, have their hair and nails trimmed and their ears cleaned, and leave the house clear for the women.

By eight o'clock, an old aunt had trickled henna paste in lacy black patterns of ferns and flowers all over Chandra's hands and feet. She had to sit quite still for two hours for it to set its colour to a strong red. Nani sat throned in the best folding chair, overseeing all the preparations amid a crowd of about forty aunts and cousins and friends.

The groom's small, skinny mother, his sisters, and sisters-in-law arrived, gleaming in heavy gold jewellery and red saris, determined not to be outshone by all the city women. They were welcomed with marigold garlands and sweets. Chandra touched the ladies' feet with deep respect, was inspected all over again and allowed to be not too bad. Nani could scarcely speak to them, for they spoke Rajasthani, and little of the Hindi or Urdu of Delhi. However, mata had learned quite a lot of her husband's native language, and Chandra could speak it reasonably well; they managed. They gave Chandra a ring from a woman who had died before her husband, to bring Chandra the same good luck.

Everyone had brought money or food. 'May you be the mother of a hundred sons! Please, a little gift to help with

16

the feast!' They perched cross-legged in elegant rows on the wide wooden beds in the living-room and the boys' room, preening, chattering and laughing like gaudy parrots. Half a dozen little girls, their western-style party dresses bright and frilly as satin lampshades, were kept occupied carrying round trays of sweets and spiced nuts, while Chandra's mother oh-so-modestly offered her guests 'Mango juice, Thumbs Up or Pepsi, just as you like, with ice from our own refrigerator.'

Chandra sat dazed, her eyes huge with tiredness, excitement, and fright, as she was prepared for her wedding. Everyone commented freely.

'How pale, how beautiful!'

'Pin her hair higher.'

'The kohl under her left eye's smudged.'

'Ai, that bright lipstick and nail varnish, accha!'

'Urvashi and I brought this Chanel No. 5, from all her school friends—smell it!'

'More red on the parting of her hair!'

'Isn't she tall!'

'A row of white and red flowers painted across her forehead, now . . . Beautiful!'

'A drop of belladonna to make her eyes wide and dark—accha!'

The graceful folds of her sari were arranged. 'Accha, the red of Durga herself! And how deep the gold fringe is!'

Last of all, nani took out the roll of black silk, to a chorus of admiration. 'Her jewellery—ai-ai! Wonderful! What a lucky girl!'

Yes, Chandra thought. She must be, surely . . . She felt empty.

At twelve o'clock, the women clapped in satisfaction. There! Wasn't she as lovely as Parvati herself, goddess of beauty? Then they hid her, draping the free end of her sari modestly down to her chin. The fabric was so fine her dark eyes gleamed through it; she could see fairly well, in spite of the belladonna blurring her vision.

A band of flutes, trumpets and drums started up in the street outside. The women applauded again. 'How bright and smart, in yellow uniforms and gold braid, and so loud! The whole of Delhi will know there is a wedding!'

Nani led them singing and laughing down the dark, narrow stair, stained with pan juice and smelling of urine in spite of all the scrubbing and incense. Every soul in the area crowded along the road or clustered at their windows to cheer and wish Chandra happiness and many sons as the women walked and danced along the street behind the band. Three sacred cows wandered across in front of the procession; 'Ai, what a sign of good fortune!' A band of gypsy musicians were welcomed into the throng; they were lucky, too, and would dance for the party later, for a small fee.

The wedding room was long, with yellow walls, a cement floor painted orange, and a curtain of blue and silver tinsel streamers looped up over the open front to make a wide archway out to the street. Along each side stood a row of scarlet stacking chairs. At the far end a picture of Ganesha, god of marriage, garlanded with marigolds, hung on the wall behind a low platform with orange and gold cushions on a crimson carpet, slightly worn but rich. A brahmin in a white robe was kneeling in prayer behind a small brazier. As the women bent to touch his feet he lifted marigold garlands from a pile beside him to hang round their necks, and pressed a mark of vermilion paste and a few grains of rice on their foreheads as a sign of blessing.

Chandra's father and brothers stood by the door, already blessed and garlanded, and more family and friends arrived. The band trotted off to the small hotel where the bridegroom was staying, while Chandra's mother and aunts offered round more cold drinks. Only three hours late; they were in good time.

Chandra peered round. Everyone was so smart! They all had new clothes, brilliant saris, crisply-pressed dark trousers and white shirts, and bapa was almost unrecognizable in a fine red turban. She jumped as mata hissed in her ear. 'Head down! Look modest! You'll disgrace us all, gawping like that!'

Quite soon the band was heard again, leading the procession of the bridegroom and the men of his family. Everyone nodded approval. 'Traditional style, look, a white horse with red velvet saddlecloth, not a taxi! And a boy attendant, in a turban!'

One old man sneered, 'But can he control his horse in Delhi traffic?' Apparently he could; they smiled with pleasure when the young man dismounted rather than falling off.

While bapa stepped forward, hiding his limp, to help the priest welcome and bless the newcomers, Chandra tried to squint up cautiously, keeping her head modestly down, but all she could see of her bridegroom Roop as he mounted the platform was his tunic of crimson silk with its gold sash, and his sparkling white trousers. He folded cross-legged on to the cushion beside her, on her left, facing down the room. His hands were small and plump. His father was carrying a sabre in a red velvet scabbard; it clanked as he sat down behind them. The priest knelt to one side, chanting, and Chandra's parents on the other. Men on the right, women on the left, the guests settled in the chairs and on the mats on the floor. The curtain at the door was lowered, to cut off the crowds of beggars and onlookers outside, and the wedding began.

Of the next four hours, the only thing that Chandra could ever remember clearly was the sweat trickling down her spine. The guests, especially the children, as they grew weary or bored got up and strolled about, chatted, had a cold Pepsi. She and Roop sat motionless while incense sticks by the handful were burned and the brahmin chanted prayers to Ganesha, god of good fortune, remover of obstacles.

She knew what to do, of course; she'd been at dozens of family weddings since she was a baby. At the right times she and Roop said prayers and threw offerings of rice,

19

ghee, and perfume into the flames of the brazier, symbol of Agni, the god of fire, of truth and purity, who presides over all great events in a person's life. They put garlands round each other's necks, and were sprinkled with holy Ganges water. Her father took her hand and put it in the groom's, with sacred mehendi leaves for added blessing clasped between, and their wrists were joined with a strip of consecrated ribbon.

At last the final ceremony arrived. They rose to their feet, her mother helping Chandra up, for she was stiff with sitting for so long. In a blare of trumpets and drums, a chorus of chanted prayers and blessings, Roop led her seven times clockwise round the sacred fire. When they sat down again, she sat on her husband's left; she was married.

As the female guests left to fetch the feast that had been prepared, Chandra and Roop were led off to a side office to sign the certificate of marriage. Their fathers went out. For the first time they were alone.

Chandra stood paralysed, staring at her feet. She was bound for life to this young man. What was he like? What would he say? What would he do?

Nothing happened. She stole a glance at him. Sangeeta would be disappointed. He was ordinary, like any of the boys in the senior school, but his round, cheerful face was pale and shiny with sweat; he looked exhausted. He'd had a long journey the day before, of course.

'Are you all right?' she asked, forgetting her own weariness, and repeated it in Rajasthani. 'Here, sit down!' In kindly alarm, she tossed back her sari, and poured a cup of water for him. Roop drank thirstily, and eased his heavy red turban up from his forehead. 'Ai, what a mark it's left on your forehead!' She stopped. Should she have criticized the turban? Bapa didn't usually wear one. Oh, dear. Had she offended him already?

Roop drank again. 'Thank you. Ah, that's better.' He smiled slightly as he looked up at her, and she realized that he was as nervous as she was. 'I think you'll be a good wife.'

She blushed. 'I'll try.'

He poured water for her. 'Here. You must be thirsty too.' He was nice, kind and thoughtful, Chandra thought, as she sipped in her turn.

He was still smiling. 'Drink up. There's hours yet to get through!'

Shyly, she smiled back. 'We should be glad we're not middle-class. The wedding might have lasted five days.'

'I'd have died!' He laughed with her. 'You know, you're much prettier than your photo! I didn't know I'd be this lucky.'

Nothing could have charmed her more. She hurried to please him, in return. 'You look much better than your photo, too. Er . . . Mata let me see it. I hope you don't mind?'

He laughed. 'No! But don't tell my father, he'd be shocked.'

Chandra sighed with pure happiness. He really was nice! 'You aren't the only lucky one, I think.'

'Ai! Wait till I beat you twice a day, and then say that!'

'That's a joke, isn't it?' Grinning, he nodded. She shook her head, suddenly serious. 'No. I mean it. I am lucky. I'll be happy with you. And I'll try to make you happy too.'

'I'm sure you'll succeed.' He patted her hand, and then in embarrassment at the show of affection, hastily took another drink of water and changed the subject. 'I'm going to own a hotel, did you know? After training college I'll be an assistant manager for two years, and then a manager, and then my family will buy a small hotel for me. That's what we'll use your dowry for.'

She nodded. 'Bapa told me. I'm very good at English.'

'Accha! Learn French, too, and Japanese, if you can. Then you can be my receptionist. Westerners like to see a woman as a receptionist, it shows you're up-to-date and modern.'

21

'And are you?' She hoped he could take a joke . . .

'Yes,' he assured her firmly. 'Don't worry—' he hesitated, giggled, and firmly declared, 'wife! Things are changing. I am definitely modern!'

She had actually wanted to be an engineer. Oh, well. He was her husband, and her duty was to help and obey him. But . . . She firmed her chin. 'Then will you do one thing for me?'

'What, wife?' He giggled again. 'Buy you lots of saris?'

Men! She shook her head. 'Call me Chandra. My name is Chandra. Remember my name, not just that I am your wife. Please.'

Slowly, the young man nodded. 'All right. Chandra. It will be very modern!' He looked as if he might actually kiss her, like in European films, but as she started to shrink back—enough was enough!—his father came in, small and wiry, his bushy grey moustache bristling suspiciously below his enormous red turban. Roop jumped back, blushing.

The old man frowned at them, especially at Chandra. What could be wrong—ah! She hastily pulled her sari forward to hide her face again, and bent to touch his feet respectfully, murmuring, 'Father-in-law-ji!'

The old man merely grunted as he touched her head in reply. 'Son, the feast is ready!' he said. Roop smiled nervously, set his turban straight, and left without another glance at Chandra. Oh, dear!

The floor of the long room had been covered with tablecloths and bedspreads. It was crowded with bowls and plates, and the women were already serving their menfolk. Platters piled with rice and chapattis, puris, and even expensive, tasteless western-style bread, with seven kinds of spicy meat and vegetable dishes. More sweets, some bought, not made, with silver foil on them. Side dishes of tomatoes, onions, cucumbers, with cooling curd. Chandra sighed as she sat down again. She and her mother and aunts had been busy for days preparing it all. And now she felt so weary she couldn't eat a thing . . .

After five hours it was time for her husband to go back to his hotel. They hadn't been able to exchange a single word in the din of the feast, but now the band and all the men went to form a procession outside. As Roop and Chandra rose, he smiled at her. 'It's hot in Jaisalmer in summer. Everybody who can, gets away. But you're to come to visit us to celebrate the Diwali festival in October. I'll meet you at the bus station.' He took her hands, speaking loudly. 'Goodbye until then, girl.' Her eyes gleamed up through the silk of her sari. He chuckled. 'Goodbye, Chandra!' he whispered, and winked.

'Farewell, my lord,' she said clearly, as she should; and added in a whisper, as she sank down to touch his feet in respect, ' 'Bye, Roop!' He stiffened for a moment. Had she gone too far? But then he chuckled again, quietly, as he touched her head.

Nani had been right; he was reared traditionally. But great-aunt was right, too. He was modern-minded. Her father had chosen well for her. They'd be very happy together, she was sure.

CHAPTER 4

Jaisalmer

At the end of September, when her school closed for the Diwali holiday, Chandra packed three cases with her wedding sari and presents—though not her jewellery, in case it was stolen—and set off on the twenty-hour journey to Jaisalmer to visit her husband's parents, all alone.

Her parents and brothers, Sangeeta and Urvashi, and a dozen of her school friends came to the bus station to see her off. Mata had been very upset for the last three days, even more emotional than usual, her round face crumpled and swollen with weeping all night. 'Mata, don't cry! I'll be back in two weeks!' Chandra assured her. That only produced more wailing. 'Look, mata, I've got everything—water-flask, and food, and my ticket. You'd think I was going away for ever! I'll be back soon, I promise!' More tears. Everybody was watching. Urvashi was patting mata's shoulder to calm her down, without much success. Chandra was surprised to find that mata really loved her so much; she'd always seemed to prefer the boys, as was only natural. It was a lovely feeling.

Even snappier than usual, bapa expressed his tension in super-efficiency. 'Deepak, get your sister four bananas and six oranges. Kirpal, climb on the roof and see that her cases and bags are solidly chained on. Accha! Don't lose the key to the padlock, beti. Don't get left behind at the stops.' He nodded to the group of girls. 'It was thoughtful of you to come and see her off. I must get back to the bank. Kirpal, Deepak, see your mata home safe. May the gods . . . ' he hesitated ' . . . give you contentment, beti. Behave yourself obediently to your new family. I may not be as rich as my cousin, but we are all Rajputs. We have honour, and pride! Do your duty, as a good girl should, and never shame us!'

24

'No, bapa-ji, I mean yes.' Flustered by her father, as usual, Chandra bowed to touch his feet. Some lads sneered, but an older man nodded approval.

Her father hesitated, smoothing his thin moustache with a long forefinger, and then hugged Chandra briefly. 'Be as good a daughter to them as you've been to me.' What? Chandra almost gaped. Bapa never praised her! He was already striding away through the crowds, brushing at his face. He couldn't be crying, could he?

Her brothers wished her good luck. She didn't know them very well. Kirpal was six years older, and Deepak four; they went to a different school, and had their own friends, besides being boys, of course. But they were her family. She said goodbye to them with love, and hugged her friends and mata, who started wailing all over again. Sangeeta put an arm round mata's shoulders for support, and made a sympathetic face—really, it was embarrassing! But comforting to have such close, loving friends.

Hastily, Chandra climbed up into the bus in time to sit by the window in a double seat, while the bus filled, and filled, and filled some more. At last, the driver climbed aboard through the little door that said 'PILOT' above a picture of an aeroplane. The conductor shoved in the last five or six people, climbed on to the step, banged the side of the bus, Chandra waved to her family and friends, they all waved back and she was off. Ai-ai, how exciting! And how scary!

For most of the twenty hours she was squashed up three or four in the double seat, but that was normal, and it was cool by the open window in the heat of the day. For the first few hours she took a blind four year old on her lap, even though he was low-caste. His mother, patiently nursing her latest baby, told Chandra how she had brought the boy to Delhi in hope of a cure, but the hospital fees were too high. After they got off, two Jain nuns filled the seat, their white robes and face-masks dazzlingly white. One snored all night.

When the sun rose Chandra peered through the dusty windows at a flat yellow desert of gravel and sand, under a high white sky. The wide emptiness frightened her. Here and there a rocky gully a metre deep showed where rain—there must be rain sometimes—had cut a jagged scar into the gravel. Thin, grey-green thorn bushes straggled and struggled up through the sand. Every few kilometres a gauzy haze of dust rose above boys driving out cream and brown cows or goats to graze from clusters of tiny houses, yellow, white or orange-painted, with roofs of corrugated iron or thatch, huddled among sparse trees and patches of green-tinted fields.

Occasionally, among the lorries and buses, they passed a cart drawn by a tall, sneering camel, its driver perched high on a load of bulging sacks above the long curved shafts. Many of the men wore the huge Rajput turban of pink, scarlet or gold. The few women to be seen didn't wear saris, or kameez and salwar like Chandra, but skirts and short-sleeved blouses of bright red, orange, pink or yellow. They draped their long veils over their heads to hide their faces as deeply as any Delhi bride. Tradition . . .

Despite the baking heat she felt shivery. She was alone. Would her new parents-in-law treat her well? But Roop would keep her safe.

A fortress grew from the horizon ahead, with towers and walls like cliffs; Jaisalmer fort. Below it, houses three or four storeys high, many hotels, small shops, narrow streets crowded with tourists, cows, jeeps, goats, dogs, street traders. Almost familiar; white and yellow, not grey and black, but it was a town, at least.

When the bus stopped, she battled through the crowd of jeep-drivers looking for tourists, to see that the men who had travelled on the roof handed down all her baggage safely. Roop wasn't there, but he shouldn't be long . . .

Five hours later, as she was getting desperate, a camel drew a cart loaded with big cans into the bus station and swayed to a stop in front of her. 'Are you the daughter of Vijay

26

Sharma?' The driver had to lean down and repeat the question before she caught his accent and nodded eagerly. Before she could speak, he said, 'I'm your brother-in-law Ashish. I've come to fetch you. Get your baggage on the cart—and veil your face, shameless!'

Chandra bit her lip as she adjusted her dupatta over her head. Oh, dear, she'd upset the family already! And the scarf was too narrow to hide her face properly . . . He didn't get down to help her with her cases, but she finally got them up on top of the tins of cooking oil and jammed safe. 'I meant to change into my wedding sari, brother-in-law, to honour my parents-in-law, but I was afraid to leave my things in case they were stolen,' she apologized while she was heaving them up.

He snorted. 'You think we are thieves here, like city people?' Oh, dear! 'Get on!' He gestured with his head for her to climb aboard, and the camel strode forward even as she scrambled up at the back.

The ride was long and slow, not like the scurry of an auto-rickshaw or the crush of the bus. The cart rocked gently with the camel's stately stride, out along a narrow road beyond the houses, past a deep half-empty tank of water with old tombs among the trees round it, and away out into the desert. Chandra leaned forward two or three times to talk to the driver. 'Where's Roop? Has he a holiday job in a hotel?' He just waved her away as if she were a mosquito. Shrugging, she settled as comfortably as she could on to her cases, and dozed.

After three hours, at sunset, the cart turned off the road, jolted along a track for another hour, and started winding among low buildings. Chandra peered in the light of the rising moon at thorn fences and high mud walls, a few lit windows faint among the black shadows. Dogs yapped as the camel swung into the yard before a house, and stopped with a gurgle of relief by a gate. Somewhere, women were wailing. Chandra took a deep breath. She'd arrived. Now to meet Roop again, and his father and mother . . .

27

Roop's father stalked out of the house, his red turban bright in the light of an electric light bulb above the door, followed by three younger men. Chandra dropped stiffly to the ground and hurried to touch his feet, murmuring, 'Namaste, father-in-law-ji!'

He didn't answer her greeting. Above her head he grunted, 'Come,' and turned away. Head humbly bowed, she followed him. Oh, dear! Where was Roop?

She was led straight through two rooms—a small shop and a bedroom, she just had time to notice—and out into another yard lit by a paraffin lamp. It was crowded with pots, goats, hens, baskets, a spinning wheel that she tripped over in the shadows. From the dark came women's voices, mourning.

A woman shrieked, 'Ai! Ai! The unlucky one! Let me tear the eyes from her! Let me rip out her hair, the demon, the devil!' Chandra shrank away from a small woman scrambling from a black doorway towards her, unveiled, her hair hanging and covered in dirt. She barely recognized her mother-in-law, moaning, 'Ai, my son! My son! Why did you marry such a snake? My son!'

She hit out at Chandra, slapping her, reaching to claw at her eyes. Chandra tried to duck away. The men behind her didn't move to let her pass. When she tried to defend herself the men hit her hands down, with shocked exclamations. She dropped to her knees, crouched down, covered her face with her arms and cowered away while the woman beat at her. After a long while, a couple of younger women came forward to catch the old woman's arms and pull her away, still screaming and tugging back towards Chandra.

Chandra was sobbing. 'What's wrong? Where's my husband? Where's Roop?'

The old man stared at her, his mouth working under his bushy moustache. 'Roop?' he said bitterly. 'He died. A week ago. A fever. My son, my youngest son. He's dead.' The women wailed from the darkness. Exhausted and horrified, Chandra knew that they were grieving for Roop's father, not her.

Cursed, struck, and spat on by everyone, she screamed, begged, wept . . . By the time she was shoved through a doorway and left alone she was half unconscious. She curled into a ball, crying as quietly as she could. Oh, Roop!

Roop was dead. At eleven years old, she was a widow.

Outside, the women of the house were still crying in their mourning. Every now and again, one would burst into the room and take a few more swipes at Chandra, cursing her for killing her husband. She didn't blame them, in their grief. Roop had lived, until he married her; it must be her fault. The traditionally-brought-up half of her accepted that, even while the educated half insisted that no, it wasn't true, she'd done nothing . . .

After a while, when no one had come to beat her for some time, she tried to straighten out. They had hit her with sticks, and thorny branches. Some of her hair had been pulled out. She licked blood from the scratches. Durga, protect her! Oh, mata, bapa! She was so wretched!

She hadn't had a drink since leaving the bus station. Was there any water here? Moonlight glimmered through a window, a fifteen-centimetre hole in the thick wall about a metre from the ground. Aching, she felt her way round the room. It was small, less than three metres square. A string charpoy bed filled one end. A quilted cotton blanket. Bags hung on nails in the mud brick wall. A metal box for clothes to keep ants out. Above the bed a shelf, with a fancy carved rim to stop things falling off. A candle and matches—dare she light it? Better not. A comb, a small mirror, scissors. Bottles; scent, oil. A metal cup. Knitting wool. At last, a flask to keep water cool . . . empty.

She was so exhausted, she couldn't cry any more. It was quite cool, even cold, in the night. Did she dare use the bed? It must belong to one of the women of the house; better not. She wrapped her dupatta round her shoulders, curled up on the floor and fell asleep.

A few minutes later an old woman came in. She bent over the little girl twitching and moaning quietly in the corner, but didn't waken her. Poor child! Poor, poor child! She spread a cloth over Chandra, to keep off the dawn chill, and stiffly lay down on the charpoy to sleep.

CHAPTER 5

The Widow

In the dark before dawn, Chandra startled awake. Someone was shaking her shoulder. She moaned as her wounds screamed in pain. A gentle voice whispered, 'Hush!' A steel cup of water was held to her lips, and she drank greedily. 'Sh! Quiet! You need to pass water? Here.' A metal pot was given to her. 'I'll empty it for you. Now, stay in here, keep quiet. You understand?'

'Shiva bless you for the water, aunty! But who are you?'

The dim figure looming above her sighed. 'A widow like yourself, child, for thirty years.' At a sound of voices outside in the yard, the woman stiffened. 'I must go. I'll bring you food. The oil in this bottle—' she put it in Chandra's hands '—use it on your bruises. Not too much,' she warned anxiously. 'If it's seen or smelt I'll be scolded for kindness to you. Quiet, now! You mustn't be seen.' The door curtain blinked, and she was gone.

Chandra sat still for long minutes, as dawn sunlight flooded in through the little window. Her husband was dead. Roop. The nice, ordinary young man, kind and cheerful, and modern; what would happen to her now? Slowly, wincing, she peeled off her torn, dirty kameez and began to rub the oil on her skin.

Tradition . . . By tradition, a widow was unlucky, accursed. She was shut away in a back room or behind a curtain, for sometimes two years. She might have to beg for her food in the streets. She wore mourning white, often old sun-bleached rags. She could never remarry, but had to serve her husband's family for the rest of her life.

No! It was illegal nowadays. They couldn't, not to her! Could they?

31

Why not? She was alone, far from home, alone in the desert. The old woman had been here for thirty years. This was what nani had been thinking of. Away out here, tradition was unbroken.

A man called sharply in Rajasthani, 'Daughter-in-law!' Roop's father. Sick with fear and hunger, Chandra pulled on her clothes again and stepped to the door. He gestured with his stick. 'Cover your unlucky face!' Hastily she draped her dupatta over her head, as far forward as the narrow cloth would go, before returning to the doorway, her hands clenched to hide their shaking. 'That's better. You are a widow. Do you know how to behave?'

'Yes, father-in-law. I must stay inside till it's time for me to go home.' She bit her lip, hoping . . .

'Home? Ha!' He barked with contempt. 'This is your home.'

'But I've another six years at school—'

'School? Why should you go to school?'

'I can get a job—'

'Job? Shiva preserve us! No woman of my family will ever shame me by going outside to be stared at by every man in town, or working as if her menfolk can't afford to keep her. And why should we pay school fees for you? You'll stay secluded in purdah, and serve us. Follow custom.' He nodded decisively, his bushy grey moustache twitching as his mouth shut tight.

Behind him his wife's voice shrilled, 'Too late for sati, even if she'd do it—no courage, modern girls! No tradition, no pride!'

Chandra shuddered. Burn herself on her husband's funeral pyre, to prove her devotion to him? A girl had done it, just a few years ago. Some people said it was her own choice, others that the family had forced her on to the fire. At least, with Roop's body burned already, they couldn't expect that of her. Desperately she protested, 'It's against the law, Miss Kapoor told us about it! You can't keep me here!'

32

'What?' The silver-headed cane lashed across her shoulders. 'Insolent! In my own house, I am the law! No government can make a law that says right is wrong and wrong is right! If this Miss was your teacher, she had no business teaching you such evil ideas! You will do your duty, and obey me as custom says—and not argue!' He struck her again, while she cried out in pain and cowered away. He nodded, and the women beyond him murmured in satisfaction. 'Accha! And how will you leave, eh? Walk across the desert? You'd die of thirst, or snakes. No, daughter-in-law. Here you will stay, as tradition lays down. Accept it.'

She knelt and held her hands out, begging. 'Let me go home, father-in-law! Please! My parents will be waiting—'

'Ach!' He spat in disgust. 'You are a fool, as well as unlucky. I spoke to your father by the telephone in the GPO in Jaisalmer. I told him last week. He said of course you must follow proper customs!'

Chandra's mouth fell open. Bapa had sent her here, knowing what had happened, what was going to happen! That was why he'd been so affected at the bus station . . . and mata had had to say nothing, let her go . . . Poor mata! They had sent her away, knowing . . . knowing . . . No! No!

Whimpering in despair, she watched her father-in-law stalk away across the little yard. Her bruises and the punctures and scratches of the thorn branches ached and stung; she was thirsty again already, with a long hot day ahead. For years . . . Maybe sati wouldn't be so bad, after all.

Children gathered to stand staring at her, black eyes wide, making the sign against the evil eye, until a woman chased them away. Not an old woman; one of her sisters-in-law, red-eyed from weeping, her maroon veil and orange blouse smeared with ash. 'Go in!' she spat at Chandra. 'Don't pass your bad luck on to any of us by looking at us! Hide yourself away in decency!' She brandished a stick, and Chandra hastily dragged herself back inside.

33

From then on, she sat in the darkness of the little room. She was allowed out for a few minutes in the blackness before dawn, to stumble down the stony, thorn-scattered path to the nearest fields to empty her toilet bowl and clean herself with earth, and then hustled back past the other women's blows and curses to her sheltering prison. The old widow brought her in a jar of water every morning and a plate of scraps in the evening. Otherwise she was outside the life of the farm, peeking out through the little window and past the edges of the curtain, longing for life, terrified of being seen herself.

Omparkash Sharma had a good farm, and his house was large. A ring of eight mud-brick huts joined wall to wall round an inner courtyard about nine metres in diameter, enclosing it completely, giving welcome shade somewhere all through the day. Their thick walls, under two metres high, were whitewashed or painted bright ochre, the thatch of their roofs deep and nearly flat to keep out heat, not rain. Over their doorways hung heavy curtains of black cotton, embroidered in bright colours. There was one for each married man and his family, one for the three unmarried daughters, a small one for guests, which Chandra shared with the old widow, and an open store. Mr Sharma's own room was the largest one, decorated with painted flower patterns and lucky swastikas in red and white round the door. It had another hut built on outside it for a small shop, where two unmarried sons slept. The narrow passage out between two huts to the outer yard had a roof-high gate which was kept locked at night. The only other way out was through Mr Sharma's bedroom and the shop.

Mr Sharma looked after the shop, gossiping for hours with his customers. His sons and labourers, and some of the workers' wives, too low-caste to go into purdah, worked in his fields, growing melons, sesame, four different kinds of grain. One man looked after Mr Sharma's camel and her calf, grooming and feeding them, and checking that their hobbles were firm every night. The Rajput women didn't need to go outside at all, because the men brought in water from the government pump in huge metal pots. They left home after breakfast, returned at sunset to be fed again, and then gathered in the shop, or outside in the cool of the yard, to relax, smoke, chew pan, and discuss the affairs of the village.

The farm workers' sons of six to ten years old, too young yet to labour in the fields, took it in turns to go to the village school with the Sharma boys or to lead out the twenty-two cows and forty goats at dawn for long days lazing in the shade, while happy, chattering gangs of their younger brothers and sisters collected cow-dung and made it into little loaf-shaped pats to dry for fuel.

All the women, Chandra's sisters-in-law and the wives of the farm workers, and the older girls, worked from before dawn till after sunset, enclosed in the yard. They cleaned, swept, burnished pots and dishes with sand, prepared vegetables, ground grain, cooked in turn on the little earthen stove built in a corner of the yard, washed clothes and babies, fed the hens, mended clothing, embroidered blouses with gold thread, spun thread of camel-hair and cotton, picked over dried beans and grain for weevils or stones. Occasionally, if a child was ill, perhaps, or on a birthday, they visited or were visited by women of the other high-caste houses in the village.

A dozen toddlers played happily all over the yard among the hens and the young goats, laughing and squabbling, crying and being comforted, indulged by everyone. It was the great relaxation and joy of the women to sit and play with the babies, telling them long, long stories of gods and heroes and clever animals. And sometimes Chandra could hear a gentle scolding, 'Ah, don't hit your brother, little monkey! Or the bad woman in the hut will get you!'

Bad woman in the hut . . . ?

35

It was herself.

Every morning and evening the women of the household did pooja. They lit the holy lamp at the base of the gnarled old tree that shaded the yard, made offerings of milk and flowers to the Shiva stone among its roots, and walked round and round it, praying for the soul of Roop and the well-being of the family.

For the happy festival of lights, Diwali, that Chandra had come to celebrate with them, they did as custom dictated. They painted the footprints of Vishnu on their doorstep to invite the god to enter, and lit tiny oil lamps on every flat surface; the men brought in new clothes, skirts and blouses, shirts and shorts, for the whole family; but in their mourning, there was little of the usual rejoicing to celebrate Rama's triumphant rescue of his wife, the goddess Sita, from the demon king who had kidnapped her.

Ten days after Chandra's arrival, at dawn, the old widow brought in a big pot of water, soap, and a cloth. 'Aunty!' Chandra gasped. 'Am I going home?' Her heart sank as the old woman shook her head mournfully.

'Sh! Be silent. Poor child! Poor, poor child!'

Chandra shivered. What was happening? She was washed, combed, and scented as if for her wedding, dressed in her silky sari. Then she screamed and wept in despair as her fine gold and ruby jewellery was hung on her. On her father's own advice she hadn't packed it in case it was stolen on the bus. Her parents must have put it in one of her bags. They really had abandoned her.

Women's voices began chanting a long pooja in the yard. Chandra was led out, the old woman supporting her, for her legs were trembling. All the women of the village were gathered, from her mother-in-law staring malevolently, down to the youngest baby blinking smiling in its mother's arms. Chandra had to stand, crying, while they stripped off her jewellery and gave it to her mother-in-law. They tugged off her gold-trimmed sari and blouse, and her fine cotton

36

petticoat, and gave her an old, faded skirt and blouse, dirty and ragged and too big for her. They pulled her hair out from its new plaits, and tossed ashes all over her, over her face and into her hair.

Her mother-in-law stood forward, her face twisted with bitter hatred. 'You killed my son. Now you'll mourn properly!' she snarled. 'You're unclean, unlucky! Your sight carries misfortune. Keep away from us, sit and pray, and do penance for the sins that killed your husband, until you've purified yourself, and we can let you come near us!' She wailed in her grief that was still keen. 'It will be a long, long time! Ah, my son! My baba!'

Chandra was pushed back into the hut.

From then on, the family ignored her, except for automatic curses as they passed her door. She sat, day after day, night after night, in heat and cold, thirst and half-starvation, staring dully, praying, weeping.

She nearly went mad.

CHAPTER 6

Durga

The old widow worried about Chandra. Poor child, just sitting staring into the darkest corner, not eating, withering away! Every evening, when she brought Chandra her grudged ration of water and food, she whispered support, trying without much success to bring comfort too. 'Ai-ai, I know what it's like, child, the suffering, it's terrible, I know, I know, but life goes on.'

Life? Chandra's young husband was dead, she was betrayed by her parents, imprisoned, alone, enslaved, half dead of thirst and starvation. What life?

'It's not all bad, being a widow,' the old woman mused one night, nodding rhythmically as she sat cross-legged on her charpoy while Chandra ate. 'At least you don't have the bother of a husband.'

'Bother?' Dully picking at the burnt chapatti and scraps of potato in her bowl, Chandra blinked slowly. 'Bother? Mata says—said—a husband is the aim of every woman's life.'

Aha! The old lady kept talking, nursing the spark of interest. 'Ji haa, ji haa. What life does a woman have without one? But a man can be trouble, too, child. A good man will be kind, and earn many rupees, and give you a good house, and sons to care for you when you're old, but how many men are good men? Even the wisest of parents may not choose well for you, and once you're wed, what can you do but obey him, even if he beats you, or wastes all his money, or gambles, or gets drunk, or is lazy-crazy?'

Chandra roused herself to answer. 'Mata said it's woman's pride and honour that however bad her husband may be she won't break her vows.' She quoted the words her father often beat into her mother. ' "A husband must be constantly worshipped as a god by a faithful wife." Nani's grandmother used to make pooja to her husband, every morning.'

'Accha, accha!' The old woman clucked approval. 'A woman must bear her life with patience and resignation, and love her husband and work and care for him, and be grateful for the food and clothes he gives her, it's her duty.' Her soft, almost whiny tone became tart for a moment. 'Besides, he'll beat her if she doesn't. Ai! A woman's life is hard, hard.'

Chandra couldn't help nodding agreement. That was certainly true. Besides, Miss Kapoor—how distant school seemed already, and it was only—what—three weeks? Four?—Miss Kapoor had said it, too, and something else. What was it? With more interest than she'd had half an hour before, Chandra tried to remember . . .

Wearily, the widow eased her back and sighed. 'If you have sons, you get respect even from your mother-in-law, and daughters-in-law come to serve you in your turn, but if you haven't . . . Ai-ai!' She mourned gently. 'My husband was the elder brother of your father-in-law. He was slow, not clever, but reliable . . . I had no son, just a beti, not yet one year old, a neat-sweet baba, my little Parvati, ai-ai . . . One month after my husband died, she fell sick, and the village nurse wasn't due for eleven days, and my father-in-law wouldn't let a man take time from the harvesting to drive me into Jaisalmer to the doctor, nor give me rupees to pay him, anyway. We tried everything we knew, all the women of the village, but . . . '

'She died?' Chandra whispered.

'She was only a girl. And she'd need a dowry later.'

'But that's . . . that's dreadful, aunty!'

'A son's a blessing, a daughter's a curse. Ai-ai!' The old lady wailed under her breath. 'I wished I could make sati then. Truly, what had I to live for? But things got better. My sister-in-law liked me and pitied me, and she treats me well. I can use this guest room as my own, and I get clothes and food just like the rest, and you'll be the same—'

'Nahi, nahi!' Chandra interrupted. 'She blames me for Roop's death. She hates me. She'll never treat me well, not in a lakh of years, aunty. Ai, I want to go home! I want to go home!'

'Home? Nahi, nahi,' the older woman said mournfully. 'Your father won't take you in, niece, even if he loves you, he can't. Tradition forbids it. Your duty is to stay here. You're here for all of your life. Accept it, you can do nothing else, and the gods will reward you in your next life.'

Poor child . . . But it would be wrong to give her false hope; better to advise resignation. Sighing, she rolled back on the squeaking strings of the charpoy and pulled the blanket over her head. After a while, gentle snores showed she was asleep.

Chandra lay awake for hours. All her life she had slept on a mat on the ground; her bruises and scratches were healed; her stomach had shrunk with lack of food, till hunger no longer griped her. It wasn't discomfort that kept her awake. After the shock and horror, her brain was starting to work again.

Bapa said she must follow tradition. Tradition said, 'From the cradle to the grave a woman belongs to a man; in childhood to her father, in youth to her husband, in old age to her son'. That was what bapa said, and mata too, who of course wouldn't argue with bapa. But Miss Kapoor, the educated teacher, said, 'Think for yourself. You have rights as well as duties.' And so did nani, an intelligent, educated middle-class lady. Should she believe them, or her aunty here, the poor country widow, ignorant and frightened? When even she seemed to despise men, obey them from habit and fear, rather than respect?

What should she do? Accept it? Live and die here? Or . . . what?

40

She thought about her school days, and a figure came into her mind. One of the great heroes of her country. Lakshmi Bai, Rani of Jhansi, had led her people against the British in the First War of Independence, that the British called the Mutiny. She had put on armour, and died fighting for her freedom. Chandra shivered. Had she courage to do that? Not to die, she didn't really think that was likely, but to dare so much? Do anything, risk everything to be free? Ah, Lakshmi Bai, inspire me!

She spent much of her time praying, as she had been told. Peeking out of the tiny window, she could see the family shrine in the hollow among the twisted roots of the old cineraria tree. Marigold petals were scattered over the small image of the bull Nandi, guarding the round white Shiva stone and the ten-centimetre statuette, smothered in red paint till it was almost smooth, of Shiva's son, lucky Ganesha. At dawn and dusk, when the women made their pooja, Chandra joined in. She chanted under her breath, for they beat her for spoiling their prayers with her unlucky voice if she sang aloud.

But during the long, hot, bright days, while the children played and the women worked and laughed about the house, and during the long, cool, black nights, while the family slept, she prayed alone. Day after day she did penance, kneeling or standing on one leg till her bones burned. She slipped out at night, with some of her scanty food, to prostrate herself humbly before the shrine and make her offering. The hens gobbled up the scraps; her sacrifice was accepted. Her sufferings might gain the favour of the gods . . .

She didn't make pooja to Shiva himself, nor to his son Ganesha, who had so badly failed to bless her marriage. She prayed to his wife, his female counterpart, the power of woman personified in many forms and faces. She prayed to her as Parvati, beautiful goddess of love; as Kali the Black, the fearsome fighting goddess; and specially as Durga, goddess of the home and of religion and tradition.

41

'Help me, Mother Durga, Durga Skandamata, Durga Siddhiratri, Durga Mahagauri, all the nine forms of Durga, bless me, protect me, advise me! I give you an offering. Speak to me, help me!'

Night and day she prayed, and wept, and did penance, and dreamed, day after night after day after night after day, till her head spun wildly, swooping through space and time . . .

All around, an overpowering scent of roses. The sudden coughing roar of a tiger, Durga's mount here in Rajasthan. The shaft of light from the tiny window expanded, blossomed into a huge golden light above her, filling the little room with ecstasy. Hands, golden hands emerging from the smiling glow, holding a bell, a cup, a trident, a snake, a wheel of fire, a water pot, a mace, a conch shell, offering her protection and blessing, warning and admonition. A voice, kind and loving and firm, like a teacher or a mother, ringing in her mind like trumpets of gold . . .

That evening she greeted her aunt, 'Aunty, what's your name?'

'What?' The widow had to stop and think. 'Padma. Ji haa, that's my name, Padma. I haven't thought about it for—ai, twenty years. Why?'

'Because my name is Chandra. Please call me by it.'

'Ji haa—Chandra!' Her aunt sounded puzzled. 'You sound different. And you're clean, you've combed out your hair and plaited it neatly. What is it?'

Chandra clenched her fists under the end of her ragged veil. This was the moment . . . 'Durga herself has spoken to me.'

'Durga! The great goddess! To you? Ai, a marvel!' Eyes wide, hands together in respectful prayer, Padma sank to kneel beside the girl and touch her feet in worship. 'You're blessed! What did she say? How did it happen?'

'I prayed, and I sacrificed, and I did penance, truly with all my heart. And today I heard her voice, as clear as if she was beside me. She said—' Chandra had had all afternoon to try to put it into words. 'She said tradition is good, and we should follow it, but not without thinking. Like . . . when I go to school—went to school—I climbed over a broken wall between our flats and the ones behind, and went through the passage there, and was only a hundred metres from the school gate. It was quickest and easiest—best for me. But an auto-rickshaw would have to go right round the block, and through the market—best for it. And a lorry would go wide-far, round by the main road, further but faster—best for it. Durga told me if I accepted tradition as always right, then it would be right for me to stay here. But I can't. I can't. And so, it would be wrong for me to stay. Like a lorry trying to climb the broken wall, or me walking the long flat road, both going to the same place, ji haa, but it's silly to expect us both to go by the same way.'

She looked across at Padma appealingly. 'Do you understand, aunty? I can't say it better. She didn't speak in words—just inside my head, I knew . . . ' She tried again. 'Tradition should be—I don't know—it should be something like a safe shelter, or a crutch if you're unsure of yourself, not a cage and a whip to make you do the same as everyone else. There is more to family pride than just obedience to rules. Thinking for yourself, like Miss Kapoor said, is not disgraceful. It is hurting people, and destroying, and greed, and things like that, that are shameful and wrong.' The old lady was nodding slowly. Maybe she did understand . . . 'So Durga said I may try to change my life. If I have the courage.'

Her heart nearly failed her, as her aunt hissed through her teeth in wonder and shock. What was Padma thinking? Would she betray her? Too late to stop now. 'So I'm going to try to escape. Even if my father won't take me in, nani will. She said she'd always help me. And Durga will help me.' She clasped her hands, begging. 'Aunty Padma, will you help me too?'

She had to wait a long time. The old lady was trembling, her own hands clasped in fright. 'Break tradition?' she muttered. 'Break custom? Ai-ai, terrible . . . They would—nahi, nahi! You can't . . . I can't . . . ' She clasped her bony hands over her mouth to hold in a wail of sheer terror, and clutched her veil down over her face, shuddering. Chandra was afraid to touch her, in case she screamed. She could only sit and watch as Padma fought against the solid pressure of her centuries-old, life-long beliefs. 'Durga told you this? You swear it's truth? I can't—Nahi, I can't . . . Oh, Durga aid me!' She curled up facing the wall, the bedcover over her head to hide herself away.

All that night, Chandra watched in fear and guilt as Padma tossed and turned on the charpoy. Sometimes she slept, sometimes she was awake, but she always refused to answer Chandra's pleading whisper. 'Please, aunty, what do you think? What will you do? I swear I tell you truly what Durga told me—don't betray me, aunty! What will you do? Please tell me!' There was no reply.

By dawn, Chandra was hollow-eyed and exhausted. 'Aunty, the sky is grey. You must get up, aunty. Please, what will you do? Will you help me?' If Padma told . . . Chandra cringed at the thought of the beatings she'd get.

Shuddering, Padma at last sat up. She looked ten years older than even the night before, the lines of her face drawn chisel-deep. Kneeling by the charpoy, Chandra braced herself.

Padma leaned forward to peer into Chandra's eyes. 'Niece—Chandra—can I argue with the gods? Ai, Durga protect us both!' She was tired, resigned almost. Her skinny arm slid round Chandra's shoulders, and her grey head leaned wearily on the girl's black hair. 'I'm old-done—nearly fifty. I'm ignorant, and I never went to school, and I can't read or write. True. But I'm not stupid. I've heard the young men's radio, and I know the world is changing. I didn't know the gods changed with it . . .' She drew in a deep breath to steady her soul. 'I'm afraid, I'm afraid . . . Ji haa, Chandra. I will help you.'

In the dark, the old woman and the young one hugged each other.

CHAPTER 7

Plans

To help Chandra grow strong again, Padma started to bring in extra food for her, chapattis, puris, fruit, even a shred or two of goat or chicken sometimes, because Rajputs could eat meat. It wasn't much, but better than Chandra's parents-in-law grudged her. Although she never admitted that much of it was her own food, Chandra guessed. She said nothing, either, but gratefully prayed harder than ever for good fortune and happiness for the old lady.

Each night they plotted in whispers, trying to foresee every problem. 'For you can't hope to try twice, niece. If you fail, if they catch you and bring you back, they'll beat you, so bad-hard! Even to death, maybe.'

'And you too, aunty, if they think you've helped me.' As Padma sighed and shrugged, Chandra took her hand. 'Don't worry, I'll make sure I'm not caught. But I worry about leaving you. I wish you'd escape with me.'

'Nahi, nahi!' Padma was aghast at the very suggestion. 'How would I live in a city, child, walking openly out in a street, with men all around? After being enclosed in purdah, protected all my life? I know about the Eve-teasers in Delhi—wicked-evil that they are! Besides, I don't speak Hindi. Nahi, I couldn't go!' She struggled to explain. 'For you, it is an escape. For me, it would be—I don't know—horrible! Nahi, nahi, it's impossible.'

'Ji haa, I understand.' Chandra patted Padma's worn fingers comfortingly. How poor-spirited! But she shouldn't argue with her elders, and besides, Padma was so alarmed that it wouldn't be kind to press it.

The next night, breathless with triumph, Padma displayed a bundle of tattered shorts and shirts. 'Look! I

46

said you should do some work, not eat at ease like a maharani, and my sister-in-law was quick-slick to agree. Can you darn and patch? If it's not well done, she'll beat you, so if you can't I'll—you can? Accha, good girl, Chandra! There will be plenty more, the boys are very rough-tough with their clothes.' Chandra was looking at the bundle, and at her aunt's face, in bewilderment. Padma smiled, pleased to bring good news. 'You can travel far safer-better disguised as a boy!'

'Of course! How smart! Clever as a fox you are, aunty!' Chandra nodded eagerly. 'And if I steal them, they'll not blame you.' She thrust the thought away, lifting a hand to her long, glossy plait. 'Can I wrap a cloth as a turban, to hide my hair? Nahi, I suppose not. It'll have to be cut.' Her lovely long hair . . .

Padma patted her shoulder consolingly. 'Everything has a cost, niece. And not always in rupees.'

They worried about money. 'I need some, aunty, for food or tickets.'

Padma, cross-legged beside Chandra on the charpoy, shook her head doubtfully. 'I'd give it gladly if I had any, Chandra, but none of us women ever handles rupees. It's the men who go to market in Jaisalmer, for salt or oil or supplies for the shop or medicines or new clothes or anything.'

Chandra knew that already, from her spying through the little window. She glanced aside at Padma. 'My father-in-law has money, in the shop.'

Padma almost fell off the charpoy. 'Steal it? Be a thief? Nahi! Never, never! You can't disgrace your family so!'

'It's not stealing, it's the unused return half of my bus ticket,' Chandra argued. 'Would you prefer me to beg, aunty? A Rajput begging? How would that be better?'

Reluctantly, Padma yielded the point. 'Maybe . . . But it's not in the shop. He keeps it hidden under his bed. You can't get at it, nahi, nahi.'

Chandra looked mutinous. 'I'll find a way. With Durga's help.'

47

'Don't rely on the gods. Their help is dangerous.'

Chandra stared. 'What do you mean, aunty?'

The old lady shook her head, and her voice turned to the story-teller's sing-song. 'A farmer once prayed to Vishnu, the god of water. He begged the god to send water to save his fields from drought, and his prayer was answered. Vishnu turned the whole Jumna River through his land, and swept away fields and farmer and all his family!' Padma nodded heavily. 'Gods are not people. They don't think as we do, Chandra. They have no . . . no common sense! Be wary of asking for their aid, accha?'

'Accha!' Chandra hid a smile. Poor Padma, always so timid! She was the one Durga had spoken to; she knew the goddess better.

Every night Chandra slipped out to make her pooja to keep Durga happy, and take long drinks from the huge water-pots in the yard corner. Now, on nights of good moonlight, she began to extend her outings, stealthily exploring and exercising; she could always make up her sleep during the day. The yard goats and dogs were used to her already, and scarcely bothered to stir when they heard her moving about.

It was December, the cold season. Everyone was indoors well swaddled against the cold night air, their door curtains tight drawn. In baking hot July she couldn't have dared go out, they'd have been sleeping outside for coolness.

It was dangerous enough even now. One night she tripped over a basket with a broody hen in it, and froze rigid, luckily in a shadowy corner, as a sister-in-law almost instantly peered out to investigate the outraged squawking. A dog got up to see what the woman wanted, and the woman threw a stone at it. 'Silence, son of a flea! And leave the fowls alone!' she hissed as it yelped and fled to a corner. Yawning, she stared up at the night sky for a moment, shivered, and let the curtain fall again. Chandra gasped in relief, slid back to her room, calmed Padma, and was more careful in future.

There were only two doors out. The high yard gate led to the goat and cow yards. She couldn't go that way, the disturbed animals would wake the whole village—besides, she was scared of cows. But the outside door of the shop could only be reached through her father-in-law's room. Where he and his wife slept the uneasy sleep of the old . . .

The first time that Chandra entered the room, she touched the red swastika, the good-luck sign of Ganesha, painted above the door. 'Let this be a good beginning, son of Shiva,' she whispered. 'Remove all obstacles for me. Bring good luck to me.' She sniffed bitterly. 'This time.'

She slipped past the curtain, moving it as little as she could. Her heart thundered till she feared they must hear it and wake. Slowly, her eyes adjusted to the dark. In the far corner her father-in-law snored on a charpoy. His wife was a huddled bundle of quilt on a mat on the floor beside it.

Slowly, cautiously, Chandra crept across the concrete floor, to the curtained door into the shop. This was pitch dark, except for a single shaft of light through a window even smaller than Padma's. She could just see to avoid the two young men rolled in their cotton blankets in one corner by the scales on their wooden crate, and the small shelves and pile of goods; biscuits, tins of oil, bags of salt, spices and grain, soap and blocks of washing soda, batteries for radios.

Two months ago, she thought, she'd have enjoyed this sneaking-snaking about unheard, as a great adventure, a joke. To her surprise, she realized she still did, in spite of the tension and desperate danger.

There was the door, and the lock; huge; heavy, old-fashioned. No sign of the key.

She retreated to the bedroom. The snoring of her mother-in-law, curled on her mat, was steady and regular. It might cover a small noise . . . She crept over and knelt down by the charpoy, jumping when her knees clicked loud. The money she needed was hidden under here. She reached underneath the bed—

Her mother-in-law grunted, rolled over, actually touched Chandra's ankle with her foot, shoved as she stretched . . . Chandra froze in terror . . . The old lady relaxed, curled up and began to snore again.

Chandra swallowed with difficulty. Durga aid me! Must go on . . .

Right in the corner her fingers touched a tin box. It grated on the concrete. Carefully she lifted it towards her. It touched the sagging strings above, and her father-in-law groaned . . . but didn't wake. She eased it past, and crept out into the moonlit yard, to crouch in a corner and investigate.

It was locked, too. Ah, Durga aid me!

After a minute's despair, she pulled up her courage. What had she expected? Of course it was locked. Like the door. Would Lakshmi Bai have given up so easily? So where would the keys be?

Under her father-in-law's pillow.

Grimly she returned to the bedroom, drifting to the head of the bed. Lucky her hands were small . . . Her thin fingers slid delicately under the folded cloth beneath Omparkash Sharma's head, and found metal, two small, two large. Gently, slowly, don't disturb his head, don't let the keys jingle . . . slowly . . . At last they were in her hand, and she crept to the door again.

The lock of the box clicked easily. In the moonlight, she lifted a cloth, to find bags of coins, rolls of rupee notes; her father-in-law was rich! There was plenty here to take her back to Delhi.

Beside the money were cloth bags of the household's jewellery, and a roll of black silk that she recognized. Her own, not part of her dowry; that was hers. That would go with her!

Oh, bapa, how could you do this? Or mata? To your beti? Her name was Chandra. Chandra!!

Silently she put it all back, locked the box, slid it back under the bed. It grated; she lifted it, straining her wrists. It stuck again. Nahi, that wouldn't do, it had to go right in . . .

there. She was going to try which big key opened the shop door, but her courage failed her. Don't tempt the gods; she'd done enough tonight. Her hands were shaking. She gently laid the keys beside her father-in-law's shoulder, and slipped out.

As the curtain fell behind her heels, she heard her mother-in-law snort, waken, sit up to pour water and take a drink. If she'd still been in there . . . Gratitude to Durga!

Over the next few nights, she stole the keys twice more. The biggest one fitted the shop door, but the lock was stiff and squeaky; she made three trips with Padma's bottle of oil and a crow's feather, just a touch each time, not enough to be noticeable, to make it run smoothly. She oiled the hinges as well.

One night, Padma's whisper was exultant. 'You don't need so much money after all, Chandra! I heard the young men talking today, and they gave me an idea. Go by train! On the roof! Mobs-crowds do it, you'll not be noticed, and it costs nothing! If you dare?' She was suddenly doubtful.

Chandra wasn't. She stopped stuffing spiced cauliflower into her mouth, and spluttered, 'Accha! Accha! What a smart-sharp idea, Padma! I can climb like a monkey. Well, I could at school, in gymnastics class. It'll be easy!' Her grin faded. 'I've still got to get to Jaisalmer, though. Over the desert—how far does a camel cart go in an hour? Six kilometres, maybe more? And then another plenty by road. Maybe I could get a lift.' She shrugged. 'First things first. Which track is it to the main road?'

'I don't know.'

'What?' Chandra couldn't believe it. 'You don't know how to reach the road, aunty?'

Padma's pained expression was faintly visible in the moonlight through the tiny window. 'Turn left at the gate, but then how far, or which track to follow . . . Northwards is all I know. I've not been outside the village since I arrived thirty years ago,' she protested defensively, and went on fast, as Chandra's mouth opened. 'Nahi, nahi, Chandra,

51

I'll not ask anyone. When you go, if I've asked directions, they'll remember.'

That was true, of course. 'Ah, Padma!' Chandra lifted a slice of watermelon. 'You're already helping so much, stealing good food for me, advising me—you're so brave, Padma-ji, to risk beatings for me! Like mata! Better,' she added bitterly.

Padma hesitated, and she looked shyly away. 'You are my baba, Chandra, my beti that I lost, come back again.' Her voice was husky.

Chandra's own eyes were suddenly scorching. 'I think today, or about now, is my birthday. Let me make it so. My own mother betrayed me. You be my mother for me, Padma. I'd be honoured if you called me beti.'

'Not Chandra?' Padma smiled through her tears.

'Ai, mata!' Chandra, newly twelve, took Padma's hand. 'Not to you. I'm your beti. If you please?'

That night she took the next step to freedom. She crossed her father-in-law's bedroom, stole the keys again, and slipped into the shop. She was getting almost used to this. This time, the lock turned easily. The hinges were silent. She slid out into the outer yard—

The guard dog bounded at her, snarling.

Petrified, she pressed against the wall. How vicious was he? He calmed when he recognized her scent. Her heart pounding, she reached to pat him, but he ducked aside warily. Behind her, the sleepers stirred. After a few minutes, their breathing slowed and steadied again, and so did Chandra's.

She peered round in the clear starlight. To her left were the thorn-bushes that closed off the entrances to the goat and cow pens. Keep well clear of there. The right side of the yard was full of neat rows of cow-dung pats, drying out; she mustn't step on them, and leave footprints. There was a wall higher than her head all round the yard, with a gate as high directly opposite her. It was heavily padlocked, but yes, the key was on the key-ring with the others. She could get out!

Better look first. Against the wall at one side stood the camel cart, four feet high. She climbed on to it and leaned to peer over the wall.

It was as well she hadn't gone out. The village dogs outside were already padding over, whining curiously, starting to yap. They might attack her. They'd certainly bark to waken the whole village. And even if she did get past them, what then? She stared out, past the thatched houses, to the empty blue expanse of the desert beyond. Left, Padma said and she remembered vaguely; but then? If she got lost, out in the desert, or sprained an ankle, or was bitten by a snake, she'd die. How could she cross at the very least six kilometres of rocky, thorny ground in thin, worn sandals, and then maybe twenty into town? In the village here there were camels, motor bikes, a lorry, a tractor, a jeep, but she couldn't handle any of them. Especially when she didn't know the path.

Discouraged, she dropped back down. She couldn't get away. She'd never escape . . .

Angrily, she swiped her tears aside. Ach, this was nonsense! She was out of the house for the first time in three months. She had boy's clothes for safe travel; she could get her money, her jewels. Chandra meant 'the moon'; in the sky the moon was full, just rising. It was a good omen. She had Durga's favour. She would not give in. She'd got this far, in spite of everything; she'd go on fighting, she'd find a way!

CHAPTER 8

Escape

As if to reward Chandra's determination, only three days later Padma bustled in early in the evening, her eyes bright among the wrinkles of her face, her hands flapping with urgency. 'Ai, Beti, great news, bright-right news! Ashish was to drive the camel cart in to Jaisalmer this afternoon, for tomorrow's market, but one of the tyres was punctured, these boys and their bottles of Pepsi, but my brother-in-law can't complain, he's the one who sells it! Anyway, by the time they mended it, it was too late to set out today. The cart's in the front yard, all loaded, ready to go before dawn tomorrow.'

Chandra was more interested in her bowl of food. 'So?'

'Its load is hay, not sacks of grain! Loose hay, piled ten feet high!'

'Hay? You mean—' Chandra leapt to the idea. 'I can hide-ride in it!'

'Ji haa! Right into Jaisalmer! Ah, my beti, here is your chance!' At the joy on Chandra's face, Padma clamped her hands over her mouth to stop herself crying. She'd lose her beti . . . again . . .

That night, Chandra crept in one last time to lift out the keys, and the box of valuables under her father-in-law's bed. Her bus ticket had cost three hundred rupees. She took exactly half that, and her jewellery. Not a paisa more than she was due; she wasn't a thief. But this was hers!

As she slipped out, she was seized by a sudden sick shivering. Was she doing the right thing? By ages-old tradition, her duty to the gods and to her family must be to stay. Durga had said she might go, if she could. But she was no longer sure. Had she really heard the words of the

54

goddess, or just imagined what she wanted to hear? Or was she just scared? Durga, hear me, help me! If I have understood you rightly, if I should go, give me a sign!

In the room behind her, her father-in-law tossed uneasily, muttering in his sleep. Suddenly he grunted, 'Accha! Accha! Go! Go away now!' His wife woke up, patted his shoulder, soothed him back to peace, and lay down again.

'Thank you, great goddess!' Chandra bowed her head gratefully as the gentle snores started again.

Padma was rolling a blanket on her mat. 'I'll rise early, and say I thought this was you in the dark,' she whispered. 'They'll think I've taken you out to the fields, and I'll say I thought you'd go with someone else when you woke. No one will know you've left till I bring your food in the evening. You'll have a whole day to get away, and maybe the night as well before they can start a search for you.'

'Accha, mata. I'll be in Jaisalmer already, and away on the train. And they won't blame you so much.' Or beat her, maybe. Oh, dear!

Chandra put on a grey and red striped shirt and khaki shorts that she'd kept back from her mending because they fitted her well and the cloth was still strong. She didn't want it to rip as she was climbing about on the train. Her knees felt odd, open to the breeze for the first time since gymnastics at school. She'd get used to it.

Miserable but determined, Padma sniffed, 'Now your hair. Nahi, leave it in its plait. Sit down.' Chandra winced at the crunching noise of the scissors, but gritted her teeth; it would grow again. 'I'll keep it, beti,' Padma whispered. 'To help me remember you.'

'As long as they don't find it!'

'Nahi, nahi.' The old lady lifted a corner of the grass mat that kept insects and lizards from falling from the thatch on to your head, and tucked the black rope away up into the straw. 'It'll be safe there.'

55

All ready to go, in her boy's clothes, her jewellery safe inside her shirt, Chandra hesitated. 'Mata—how can I go, leave you to face them all?'

'Go on, go on!' Padma whispered urgently. 'Don't bother about me! It's after midnight, beti, they'll be rising soon. Don't waste time!' She was crying, trying not to wail. 'I love you. And so I tell you to go. I'm an old, worn-out hag. Do you want to stay, to become like me? Nahi, nahi. Go now, beti, and all the gods bless you!' She clung to Chandra, struggling against her own longing to keep the girl, afraid for her whether she went or stayed.

'Thank you, queen among women! You may be old, but you're wise, and kind, and brave! Maharani-ji! Mata! You've been the hands of Durga for me! I'll pray in thanks to you every night, I promise!' Chandra was crying too. To be called beti was so comforting! She was so scared . . . She didn't want to go . . . She must . . .

At last Padma thrust her away, to watch weeping as her beloved child crept across the yard, turned to wave goodbye, and disappeared. Then the old woman sank down on her charpoy and rocked in misery, the end of her veil stuffed in her mouth to muffle her sobbing.

For the last time, whatever happened, Chandra slid like a ghost across Mr Sharma's room, past the sleeping men and across the shop. She unlocked the door and went out, jumping as the guard dog touched the backs of her knees with its cold nose. She tried a trick that Sangeeta had seen in a film once; she tied a bit of string to a pencil and slipped the pencil through the end of the key. Durga, please . . . To her delight, it worked! When she pulled gently on the string, the key turned quietly, the pencil dropped out and she drew it under the door in triumph. They'd never know that her father-in-law hadn't just forgotten to take the keys out last night . . . She hoped.

The cart was loaded higher than the wall with hay, its long shafts leaning on an empty crate. Chandra burrowed into the fragrant, rustling fronds at the back, deep in to hide her feet. The guard dog stood on its hind legs to sniff at the breathing hole she made at the side, and then went off to curl up and go to sleep. Cosy and comfortable, and exhausted, so did Chandra.

She awoke with a jump to the squeak of the outside gate, two hours before dawn. Her brother-in-law going out for the camel; but no alarm! She'd not been discovered, so far . . . In half an hour, a grumbling camel was led into the yard by the light of a paraffin lamp. Camels don't like going backwards; the cart was tilted and tugged forward till the shafts and harness could be tied on.

Soon the men had eaten their breakfasts, and her father-in-law's voice sounded, sharply alert in spite of the early hour.

' . . . Not a paisa less, you hear? He'll claim the grass isn't tip-top quality, he always does, the Bengali swindler, but you tell him it's fit for the horses of the sun.'

Tense and trembling among the hay, Chandra prayed she wouldn't sneeze. The cart swayed as Ashish climbed up and settled on the hay; right above Chandra's head. It pressed down; she was smothering . . .

'The rice from Dharam Singh as usual, check there's no sand in it.'

'Accha, bapa.' The driver's voice rose slightly. 'Move on, then, you! Hutt!' Camels weren't as clever as dogs or horses, they never learned to answer to a name—and if she didn't get some air she'd die . . .

Chandra struggled to push herself back out from underneath her brother-in-law's weight, her movements lost in the jolting of the cart on the rutted track. Quick, before she suffocated . . . but smooth, in case he noticed the movement . . . At last she was far enough out, and could relax—but not sigh, in case the grass seeds made her choke . . .

57

The camel moaned and grunted as it heaved the cart up over a two-foot step, and then a smoother ride. The main road. Chandra's skin seethed with tickles. She was itchy all over, but on the smooth road she didn't dare scratch. Occasionally she jumped as a jeep or a lorry roared past.

When the cart reached the town its regular rocking stopped. It was stopping and starting through the traffic, jolting up and down in potholes and kerbs, stones, and rubbish as it threaded through the narrow streets. Chandra knew she must get out before it stopped and she was seen emerging. She wriggled backwards till her feet came free; a couple more shoves and wriggles, and she dropped out into sudden brightness and a shout. A man was calling to Ashish, pointing, laughing! Ashish was turning, looking for her. Terrified, half-blind in the sunshine, she dived aside round a corner, across behind two cows and a van, peered back . . . No one was chasing her. She was safely out of sight. She was away!

And at last she could scratch!

After a blissful, busy minute, she brushed herself down, shaking bits of grass out of her clothes, combing her ragged hair with her fingers. She looked very much like the other boys in the street, she decided, tattered but fairly clean. Her head felt queerly light and airy. So did her knees—she had to stop herself trying to hide them with her hands. Now, where was the station?

Before the morning train left, she just had time to get a drink of water and a wash at the public tap. It was the first time in months she had washed properly in running water, she hadn't dared steal so much from the water-jars. It was so cool, so wet . . . Reluctantly, she dragged herself away, and joined a party of men climbing up the side of the second carriage, on their way to a wedding. One of them kindly gave her a hand up the last bit—drifting about the yard hadn't kept her arm and leg muscles in trim. The train roof was high, but quite broad; she settled herself as near the middle as she could get.

A jolt, a screech of metal; at last, they were off. She was free!

She might fall off! Nahi, she could cling tight. Someone might recognize her! But no one in Jaisalmer had seen her face except in the bus station months before. As the train rocked down the line across the desert, at last, Chandra dared to relax. She was free!

A man was looking at her curiously. Why? Oh dear! Her legs were very pale, far paler than any normal poor boy's. Her face and arms, too. Stealthily she dirtied herself with soot from the train roof as camouflage. She was free!

She spoke Rajasthani with a noticeable Delhi accent. Besides, she didn't know how boys and men talked among themselves. So, while the men passed round a bottle of beer and told wedding jokes, cheerful if rather gritty in the breeze, she grinned but kept quiet. She was free, free, free . . .

She hoped Padma would be safe, not too much beaten for not noticing her escape. Oh, Durga, look after Padma, she just helped me do what you said . . . And look after me, too!

At Jodhpur in the afternoon, after eight hours roasting on the train roof in the baking sun—she'd not realized how cool the hut was—she had two hours to wait for the Delhi train. A man was kneading chapattis on a plate laid on the dusty platform, and baking them on a small stove. Ten rupees bought two of them with a spoonful of spiced lentils, three oranges and a throw-away earthenware cup of chai.

She needed to relieve herself. She couldn't do as men did, who simply turned their backs on the world in a quiet corner while people politely ignored them; nor, in her shorts, could she copy the low-caste women, the Harijans and beggars who weren't allowed into the women's loo, who squatted with dignity within the shelter of their skirts on the edge of the platform. She had to use the men's room, and tried not to blush as she queued for a cubicle, eyes firmly on the ground.

A tourist dropped an empty plastic mineral water bottle. She grabbed it almost before it hit the platform, before the local scavengers got it, and filled it at the tap. Now she'd not need to climb down to drink at stations, and maybe see the train go off without her.

But it wouldn't matter. Nothing mattered. She didn't matter. Nobody was expecting her; not a soul in the world knew who she was, or cared. Her parents had sent her away; she had lost Padma; her nani didn't know she was coming. Among the crowds on the hot grey platform, her mind swirled dizzily. She was alone, alone . . . She shivered. Who was she? What was she? A single soul, in the middle of teeming millions . . . A speck of nothing, infinitesimal, worthless . . .

No! She was Chandra! And she was free!

CHAPTER 9

The Train

On top of the Delhi train, Chandra's new neighbours were mostly thin young men and some wives heading for the city in hope of work, clutching bundles of clothes and bedding. The man next to her swung down at every stop to talk through the window to his family in the crammed carriage below. She kept his place and his bundle for him, and when she clambered wearily down at Jaipur station, six hours later at midnight, to refill her bottle and buy food, he kept her place for her in return.

He eyed her samosas longingly as he gave her a hand up again. He didn't beg, but she knew . . . He was a dark, low-caste Megwal, with a broken nose, wearing only a torn vest and a tattered lunghi wrapped round his skinny waist. To keep caste, to be properly modest, she shouldn't talk to him or touch him. But then, the idea of a properly modest Rajput girl sitting on top of a train in grubby shirt and shorts was incredible anyway. She couldn't eat much in any case, her stomach seemed to have shrunk. She offered him one of the little parcels of spicy meat.

His wide, uneven teeth gleamed white in the station lights. 'Krishna reward you, little brother!' He looked as if he'd not eaten for a week. Uncannily, he echoed her thought. 'The first food past my teeth in two days!'

'Ah? You must be starving!' They all swayed as the train moved off.

'Why else am I here? May a thousand demons with ten heads each chew Kirpan Singh's legs off fragment by fragment, and spit the bones into a pigsty!' He spat over the edge in illustration before stuffing the last scrap in and chewing luxuriously, like one of the demons he called on.

'Why? What has Kirpan Singh done to you?'

'Done? Ha!' He snorted. Everyone around, huddled in sweaters and scarves against the cold wind, was listening. 'My name is Bhawar Priya, from Raita village, near Barmer.'

'I'm . . . er . . . Chander Sher. From Gurha village, by Meerut.'

'Accha. Listen, while I tell the tale! Ten generations of my fathers were his tenants, Kirpan Singh's and his fathers'. And then I stood for election to the village council, against him. Against my landlord. My wife called me ten kinds of fool. "The bullfrog croaked that he could shout louder than the bull—until the bull stepped on him!" But I said it was my right, he couldn't stop me, the day of the tyrant zemindars was past, the law had deposed them, the world was changing. Ha! More fool I! He hired goondas, thugs, to beat up anyone who supported me. I am not a fighting man, but I tried to help a friend.' He touched his broken nose. 'So I got this!'

There was a chorus of sympathy, but he held up a hand to show he wasn't finished. 'My friends and I went to vote all together, for safety. But the clerk said we had voted already, our names were ticked off. Even mine! You know, Chander, when you vote, your hands are marked with ink so that you can't vote twice? We showed our hands, they had no ink stamp, but the clerk said we must have cleaned it off. Kirpan Singh had sent men to vote in our names! Probably bribed the pig-dog of a clerk, too! So we were cheated, and that wart on the backside of a diseased she-camel was elected again.'

Everyone exclaimed in disgust.

'It's a disgrace!'

'This is a democracy, one man one vote, not the days of the British Raj.'

'We know it happens in Bihar, but Rajasthan is civilized!'

'It shouldn't be allowed!'

Bhawar spat again. 'Ji haa! I agree with you, friend! But how to stop it, eh? He has the rupees to pay off the

62

politicians and the police, we haven't. May he and his family be consumed by red ants, and reborn as locusts—hai, who would see any difference? He raised my rent for the land, that has been in my family for ten generations, until I could no longer feed my children. No one on the farms around would offend him by hiring me. I couldn't even borrow money!' Heads were shaken; it was a hard day when the money-lenders refused to get their talons into you. He spat again. 'So, my wife died. I had no rupees for medicine—but it was hunger more than illness.'

He shrugged in bitter, baffled anger. 'So we left. I burned down my hut—he won't get that, at least! My sons are below. I sold my eating knife for ten rupees to pay their ticket. The gods blessed me with four sons in eight years—good boys, good boys, the oldest is looking after the younger ones—and up here, we'd have lost one at least before Delhi.'

Several of their neighbours chimed in with their own stories of corruption and injustice. Chandra was surprised. Even men were treated badly, it seemed.

She woke with a lurch. Bhawar was holding her arm, laughing. 'Ai, careful, Chander! You were nearly off!' Oh, dear! Chuckling, Bhawar pulled her close with a strong wiry arm and spread his thin cotton shawl round them both. 'Tuck in by me, little brother.' He was kind, warm and comforting, tough and secure. And she simply couldn't keep her eyes open . . . She tucked her shirt tighter, leaned against her new friend and slept again. She was free . . .

A jolting stop, just before dawn, woke her. Where was she? On top of the train. Safe. And yes, her money and the roll of jewels were safe too. She sat up stiffly, stretched, yawned. Scratched. Ai, not fleas? Oh, Durga! But everything had a price, even not falling off a train. It was worth it.

'Alive again, little brother?' Bhawar was grinning down at her. 'Or . . . little sister?' His voice was a murmur, his

63

eyes merry. He held up his hands as she shrank away. 'Nahi, nahi! Never fear me! Have I not eaten your food?' Smiling, he nodded reassuringly. 'It's dangerous for a girl to travel alone. I understand. Safer for a boy. Accha! Have a drink . . . Chander! We'll be in Delhi in an hour, you might as well finish it.'

He had kept her safe. And he wasn't going to betray her, or attack her, or rob her, or anything . . . 'Thank you, Bhawar, you're a good man!'

'I follow Ramakrishna.' He shrugged expansively. 'What else are we on earth for, little brother, but to help each other?'

She couldn't help giggling. 'Even Kirpan Singh?'

'That rotting jackal!' He made a face. 'You call him a man?'

Gratefully, she gave him the last of her samosas. 'What will you do in Delhi, Bhawar sahib?'

He laughed at the respectful title. 'No need to be so polite, not to me! I'll do any work-task that comes along. Do you know someone who needs a watchman, or a coolie, or anything? Ah, well. I'll find something.'

Suddenly, she found herself whispering her story. What did he think? Was what she had done really terrible?

Bhawar constantly exclaimed in sympathy, but her final question made him pause and think hard. 'I don't know,' he said, finally. 'I'm poor, but I went to government school for four years, and I know the world is changing, as your aunty does. A brave woman!' Chandra nodded, choking back a sudden prickle of tears. 'I know it's against the law, to treat widows badly. Though of course they shouldn't remarry . . . And people, especially women, should bear their troubles in this life patiently, as penance for sins in a past life, to earn a better life next time.' He scratched his bent nose. 'But then, I haven't done that, either. Ah, only the gods are perfect. Ji haa, I agree it's wrong. But for a girl to disobey her father . . . ' He shook his head with a grimace of misgiving. 'But he should treat her with care, too . . . And you say the goddess told you to go. Ach! I give up!'

He shrugged his bony shoulders. 'Your father-in-law is a landowner, a zemindar, like Kirpan Singh? Then I'm for you, girl!' Though his words were confident, his face was nervous. He'd just realized she must be high-caste, too; he'd thought her accent was unusually polite.

If a man could accept it, it wasn't so very bad, maybe . . . even a Megwal's approval was a relief.

Heat and light suddenly cheered them as the sun leapt over the flat horizon. Chandra sat relishing the life around them. This countryside was still dry and dusty, but here there was water as well, and other colours than yellow and cream under the blue sky. Boys splashed happily round shiny black buffaloes wallowing in dark water tanks, garlanded with strands of white lotus or purple water hyacinths; white egrets stalked gracefully through herds of honey-coloured cows in green fields; tall silver seed-heads swayed above the lush banks of irrigation ditches. Trees flourished, palms as well as neem trees and thorns, with blossoms of red or yellow, and wide canopies of vivid greens. On fences, bushes, stacks of dungpats beside the tracks, washermen had draped to dry long sari cloths, brilliant as sapphire, emerald, and amethyst as well as the ruby and topaz favoured in Rajasthan.

Houses became more common, more crowded. On the roads, buffalo and ox-carts, auto-rickshaws and taxis, bicycles and scooters, rickshaws and pony ekkas slowed the long-distance traffic of buses, cars, and lorries, all automatically dodging the sacred cows now lounging out on to the road. Some goats, some donkeys, even an elephant, but not a camel to be seen.

Hoardings showed posters for beer, newspapers, hotels, fridges . . . Mata was so proud of her fridge. What would she say? And bapa?

Forget that; get to nani first!

65

No fields left now, only houses and shops, flat roofs where women never glanced up from washing or cooking as the train rattled past. Cows were strolling along the track, calmly moving out of the way of the trains. At every stop, more people packed on to the train, heading for work and school. Modern multi-storey buildings appeared far ahead, and stretched up towards the sky. At last the train ran under a roof, grey with soot. New Delhi Station.

Bhawar held Chandra steady for a few seconds as the crowds of commuters swarmed off, and then helped her down. 'Goodbye, then, little brother. Safe home to your grandmother! See, here are my sons. They can stay here on the platform while I go and find a place for us.'

He was talking too much, and grinning too widely. Checking that her jewels were still safe, Chandra realized even a man could be afraid, in a new, huge world. She smiled at him. 'Thanks, Bhawar!' She'd miss him—

Someone pushed her. She tripped over a mailbag and fell. A hand grabbed at her, she felt her shirt rip, the precious bundle of her jewels dragged from her waistband. She screamed from anger more than her hurt knee. To lose them now! In a second, she was up again. Where was the khaki shirt of the thief? There! 'Stop! Stop, thief!' she cried, hobbling after him. The man was racing among the crowd, disappearing—

Bhawar charged past, yelling, 'Stop! Thief! That man there—stop him!'

A policeman at the end of the platform whipped round, his heavy bamboo stick ready. Chandra jumped up on to a luggage trolley to see better, and just glimpsed the hand-flick as her bundle was passed to a banana seller squatting beside a bookstall. The thief looked startled, slowed down, and gaped round innocently. 'Who, me? A thief? Never! It's a slander! Who says so? This black ruffian?' Bhawar grabbed him. Everybody stopped to watch as the man shouted, 'Search me! What have I stolen? Search me, constable sahib! Where is it—in my shirt? In my trouser pocket? I have nothing, see!'

Frantically Chandra limped up the other side of the wide platform, shoving among the people to stop beside the banana seller. He was furtively tucking something away under his wide metal tray. Her jewels, it must be!

'Dirty, low-caste country lout! You brown-rice jungly!' The policeman was starting to blame Bhawar for making false accusations. She had to save him—and get back her jewels! But if she was wrong . . . Please, Durga, let her be right! Chandra drew in all her courage, grabbed the edge of the tray and heaved. It clanged down, drawing all eyes round in one startled jump. 'Look!' she screeched thankfully, snatching up the cloth roll under the man's knee.

The crowd roared with anger and excitement. An army sergeant, travelling with a platoon of soldiers, yelled, 'Nab them!' and his men leapt enthusiastically to seize the thieves.

The policeman pushed back through to them. 'What is it? What's stolen?'

'My . . . my mata's jewels!' Chandra screamed above the din. 'That man—he must have seen me check they were safe, on the train! He grabbed them, and passed them to this one! Ha, constable sahib, put them in prison!'

Bhawar was shaking her arm. 'Nahi, nahi! Quiet! The police will take the jewels as evidence, and you'd never get . . . er . . . ' he glanced at the policeman 'it'd be months before you got them back! Say you made a mistake!'

Oh, Durga! But Bhawar knew more than she did. Chandra bowed to the policeman. 'I'm sorry, constable sahib, I can't be certain—'

The policeman snarled. Just a few more arrests, and he'd be made sergeant! Should he take them all in, force the boy to give evidence? He still might not get his promotion. Or take the loot and 'lose' it? But his inspector was honest.

There were the soldiers, too, as witnesses. And a ragged lad like this would only have copies, not real gold. Better a small profit than the risk of losing his job. 'You have money there, boy? Accha!' He lifted about half. 'A fee for stopping the thief, saving your trinkets. Accha?'

In her turn, Chandra hesitated. Should she make a fuss? Behind her, Bhawar was quite sure she shouldn't. 'Accha, constable sahib! Accha!' He glanced over. 'And for the sergeant also!' He handed another twenty rupees to the soldiers, and tugged Chandra back into the crowd.

The constable grinned. Fifty rupees was worth more than a doubtful promotion. Feeling good, he turned his attention to the thieves, still held by the soldiers. They mustn't get away with it! He swung his stick to crack on their shins. The crowd yelled approval; this was the proper way to deal with criminals, no time-wasting nonsense of courts and lawyers! All the bananas had vanished, crushed underfoot or lifted and stowed away quietly by the platform beggars. When the policeman tugged his shirt smooth again, nodded acknowledgement for their help to the soldiers, and stalked off, the two thieves were glad to be able to limp away instead of being thrown into prison.

Bhawar helped Chandra over to the nearest tap, nodding thanks for congratulations from the travellers around. 'Come, drink, wash your face, little brother! A good thing I was there, eh?'

Chandra pulled her torn shirt tight across her chest to hold the little bundle safe. 'Ah, Bhawar-ji! How can I thank you? And you said you weren't a brave man! You're brave-strong as Rama! Your sons must worship you!' He swelled with pride at the praise. 'Come with me to my nani's house, she can reward you more than I can. Oh, please! I'm so scared—what if they're still watching?'

'Not after the beating from the policeman!' Bhawar chuckled. But he considered it; the boy—the girl—had money and caste, and owed him a favour. There should be a good reward from the grandmother, or even a job and a place to live—it could be his chance, in this huge, strange city . . . And he liked the lad—the girl. She'd given him food, when she had little enough. And she might still be in danger. Accha. He'd stay with him—her—and see what happened!

CHAPTER 10

Nani

They settled Bhawar's sons with some puris to eat, squatting patiently in a corner of the platform to wait, and Chandra led their father towards the rows of auto-rickshaws, little three-wheeled scooter taxis. He was appalled. 'You're a maharani, little brother? To pay so much, instead of walking?'

Chandra sagged. 'Ai, Bhawar, it's a long way. I don't know the road or the buses from here, and I'm so tired and stiff—oh, come on! I still have about fifty rupees, thanks to you—let me give you a treat!'

Thrilled by the luxury, he soothed his conscience by bargaining fiercely for her with the driver. 'Forty rupees? Are we rich white tourists? Make a proper price! Thirty—still too much!' He reluctantly agreed to twenty.

As they jolted out of the station forecourt into the swirling traffic, the horn barping like a strangled duck every few seconds, he sat forward to peer out of the open sides and miss nothing of the ride. 'So many cars! Is everyone rich here? What is that, on the back of the taxi? "All God's child, obey traffic rules?" Good advice! Go on, brother, jump the red light—accha, the policeman didn't catch you! Ai, you jungly, boot your beetle-bicycle to Bombay, son of a snail, make way for your betters!' Chandra was giggling helplessly. 'What palaces of glass and stone—skyscrapers? Well-named! So many white faces! Watch out for that bus—Krishna save us!'

As the driver nicked between a bus and a lorry, laughing in superiority over the country bumpkin, Chandra soothed Bhawar. 'Don't worry! Auto-rickshaws are magical, they're

six feet wide, but they can slip through two-foot gaps!
When they have a good driver, of course.'

'Ji haa! That's right!' Flattered, the driver nodded and
grinned approval. Bhawar tried to relax his white fingers
from the rail.

To avoid the worst of the traffic, the auto-rickshaw left
the wide, straight boulevards and wriggled round the back
streets. Bhawar eyed the tattered shacks of palm-leaf
screens and cardboard that filled the empty spaces
between shabby buildings and cow-byres, and erupted
like molehills from the piles of rubbish alongside the wider
roads. Tiny cement ovens were built directly on some
pavements and the centre islands of roads, where hundreds
of families lived in the open. The only water supply for
many was from the street pumps gushing freely at some
corners, thronged with men, women, and little girls
washing themselves and their clothing openly, drawing
privacy round themselves like a cloak of invisibility,
determined to keep personally clean in spite of the city's
eternal greasy grime.

Finally he sighed. 'I've a cousin here in Delhi. Somewhere. I didn't know the city was so huge. I'd hoped to stay
with him, but . . . '

Chandra knew what he was thinking; if he couldn't find
his cousin, he and his family would be living like this,
maybe for years, maybe for ever. 'Don't fret, Bhawar,' she
assured him. 'Nani will help you find a job and a place to
live.'

'Thank you from my heart, little brother.' Bhawar smiled
widely. He certainly hoped so!

Nani lived in a good pre-war colony, an estate with garden
beds between the blocks of six-storey flats. Bright shades
on verandahs, bicycles chained to racks in front of the
houses, showed that it was a rich area. As the auto-
rickshaw manoeuvred between the parked cars, Bhawar fell

uneasily silent. When the driver demanded more money than had been agreed, he dealt with it firmly. That he could handle; but then he hung back. This wasn't his kind of place.

'Come on, Bhawar,' Chandra urged him. 'There are nani's windows, and she'll be—' She stopped.

From the dark steps at the entrance to the flats in front of her, a tall man in spotless khaki shirt and trousers was rising to his feet, striding forward. Limping forward, leaning on a stick. She put up her hands to keep him off, and screamed faintly as her father's long fingers gripped her wrists.

'Slut! Shameful, shameless! To disgrace me and my family like this! Pig! Shameless western sow! This is what comes of a modern education—you bring shame on us all! Scorpion!' At every insult, his stick cracked on her sides and shoulders. She screamed, but she couldn't fight him—he was her father . . .

Bhawar stood hesitating. A girl's father had the right to beat her—he was a high-caste Rajput—Bhawar himself was an outsider, only a Megwal, he didn't dare . . .

Children passing on their way to school started to gather, shrilling in excitement. Their parents, heading out to work, stopped too. As the crowd swelled, Chandra's father started to drag her away, still shouting insults at her. 'Hussy! Daughter of shame! To run away—to break tradition!'

'Nahi, bapa, nahi—please!' Chandra tried to break free, but he was too strong. There was a taxi waiting. If he got her into it, she'd never get away. In desperation, she screamed, 'Bhawar! Save me! Please help me!'

Bhawar yelled. He wasn't a fighter. He couldn't quite bring himself to touch the higher-caste man, to tug him away from the girl, to hit him . . . But this was Delhi, where all men were equal. And his little brother was being dragged off to slave for a zemindar . . . 'Stop! Tyrant! Bully! Stop there! Let her go! Tyrant!' He was working himself up to strike . . . if he had to . . .

Chandra's father realized it. He halted, still gripping Chandra's wrists painfully tight, and raised his stick to threaten. 'You pig's turd, stand back! Don't dare come between a father and his daughter!'

'You've no right—' Bhawar protested.

'I'm her father! Who else has any right to her!'

'She has a right to herself!' Nani was pushing through the crowd, panting from running down the stairs, her silver hair and white sari shining in the morning sunlight. 'You do not own her, Vijay Sharma! Widow slavery is illegal, and you know it! You can't send her back! They will kill her. Let her go at once!'

Round them, in the street and on the balconies, people realized what was happening. They began to murmur, then to shout angrily. A few agreed with Chandra's father, but most were furious, moving forward, starting to call out, 'Let her go! Go away, man! You have no right! Old-fashioned tyrant! This is wrong! Go away before we call the police!'

'Tradition says that—' As Chandra's father started to argue, Bhawar, encouraged by the support of the crowd and the old mem, suddenly jumped forward and waved a fist in his face. Mr Sharma flinched, lifted his stick again to protect himself—in that instant Chandra jerked her wrists free and fled to the shelter of her nani's arms.

Relieved that he hadn't needed to strike, Bhawar leapt back, still poised ready to jump between Chandra and her father at need.

Mr Sharma stood rigid, his thin face twisted with strain and anger. The crowd was cheering this low-caste lout; they'd stop him taking his daughter . . . Corrupt westernized fools! 'Accha! Accha! You want her, woman, you have her!'

At the hissing screech, everyone fell silent. His head poked forward to emphasize the words he spat at nani. 'You sent her to school, you made her what she is—a decadent western sow-bitch, with no thought for the shame she brings on her family, her country, her gods, by indulging her own selfish fancies instead of doing her duty! My beti! Accha! You want her, you have her! She's no longer my child. I'm not her father, my sons aren't her brothers, my wife isn't her mother. Her name will never be spoken again in my house. Let her eat filth, let her die in a dung-heap, let her be reborn as a beetle—I don't care! She's nothing to me! Nothing!' His face showed that he was lying. Blinded by furious tears, he spun on his heel, caught the toe of his bad foot in a hole in the pavement, and fell full length in the dust. The children around them screamed with excited, embarrassed laughter.

'Bapa!' Out of habit, Chandra darted to help him, but he angrily struck out at her to drive her away, back towards her grandmother.

A man fetched Mr Sharma's stick and supported him as he pulled himself to his feet, straightened and dusted down his clothes. His eyes were full of rage now, not tears, and his voice was choked with the humiliation. 'Laugh, then!' The children fell silent again. 'Go on, laugh! And laugh again, when she gets her due! I don't want her, but her father-in-law won't feel this way!' He eyed her bitterly, venomous as a snake. 'Watch out behind you, girl! He has sons, and nephews, and friends. Any man behind you at any moment may be one of them, come to grab-snatch you back to your duty—and may Shiva pity you then, for no one else will!'

As he stalked off towards his taxi, Chandra burst into tears. Murmuring thanks to the women who had come out to support them, nani led her into the flats. The school children and the business men and women in the crowd suddenly realized they were going to be late, and hurried off with their briefcases to their cars and scooters, while the rest stood gossiping animatedly for several minutes before heading home or out to spread the news.

Bhawar scratched his head. Would little brother remember him? Of course, sooner or later. Women needed a while to recover from a scene like that. He'd wait. The children would be all right back at the station, and he'd been promised a reward. He squatted behind the bushes near the entrance, where it was cool and shady and he'd not be seen by any officious sweeper, to snooze patiently. Ai, he'd been a lion! He wished he'd done that to Kirpan Singh!

It was almost two hours before he heard his name called, and woke with a start. 'Here, mem!' he mumbled to the girl in the green sari, stumbling to his feet and rubbing his eyes. Then he looked more closely. 'Ha, is that you, little brother? I mean—'

'Ji haa, Bhawar, it's me.' Chandra nodded, smiling. She looked different now, clean and tidy, her shaggy mop of hair neatly trimmed, wearing one of her aunt's saris in place of the torn, dirty shirt and shorts. 'I'm sorry I was so long. I was upset.' Her eyes were still swollen.

'Ai-ai, I understand, little brother—I mean mem—'

'Come along, Bhawar.' She beckoned him in. 'Don't be afraid, nani wants to thank you herself. Ji haa, come along! Come on!'

The stairs were clean and well-lit, smelling uncomfortably of antiseptic like a doctor's clinic. A heavy, polished door led to a hall with marble floor patterned in grey and white chequers, doors to more rooms, cream paint, thick green curtains, soft western chairs. This was a palace! Bhawar had to be almost dragged into the flat, very aware of his dirty, ragged lunghi and shirt, his dark skin.

In front of a glass display cabinet full of little ornaments and dolls, two ladies were sitting on a cushioned red settee. The old widow he'd seen outside was smiling gently, encouragingly. The other was younger, sharper, thinner, in a purple and black sari with a gold thread—very rich! And very annoyed at having such a low-caste coolie in her house; she was frowning, her lips tight, her eyes angry.

Palms together, he touched his fingers to his brow and bowed deeply, shoulders hunched to make himself as small as he could, his eyes fixed humbly on the green and red rug at their feet.

'Nani, Aunt Amrita, this is Bhawar. He saved me from falling off the train, as I told you, and helped me against the thieves, and the policeman, and . . . and bapa.' Chandra's voice faded on the last words.

'Namaste, Bhawar.' The old mem's voice was soft and kind.

'Namaskar, mem-ji.' He kept his head down.

'Bhawar, I have to thank you.' She nodded graciously. 'My granddaughter could have been lost-dead, certainly in very serious trouble, without your courage and kindness-goodness.' He blushed, shuffling his feet in embarrassment. He was more used to being shouted at than praised. 'How can I reward you? Money? Or a job, Chandra says? And a place to live?'

He bent to touch her fine gilded sandals, stammering his thanks. 'Give me work, maharani, and I and my family will serve you faithfully all our lives! What can I do for you—fetch the moon for your footstool?'

'Bhawar, you're a poet!' She laughed, but seemed pleased, though the other woman was snorting contempt. The old mem glanced aside at her. 'Amrita, please go to the kitchen and see what the cook can find to give this good man.' Good man! He could scarcely breathe for delight and embarrassment.

As the young woman swept out in a temper, nani turned back to her dirty, smelly, ragged visitor. Oh, dear! But she owed him a great deal. 'Accha, Bhawar, I have a very important job for you.' He dared to glance up hopefully. 'You heard Chandra's father. At least for now, she must be guarded-warded. Will you do it? I'll pay you well. What did you earn in the country?'

'Twenty rupees a day, mem,' he whispered. In fact, fifteen was as much as he'd ever got for fourteen hours' labour, and for that his wife had had to work for the farmer's wife as well; but here, things were different . . .

She smiled, fully aware that he was stretching the truth. 'Accha. Well, I'll pay you thirty.' His heart swelled in such delight, he scarcely heard the rest of what she said. 'My car is away being mended, so that my garage is empty just now. It may be days-weeks before the car comes back. You and your sons can live there until then. There is a tap in the yard, and a government school round the corner. Accha?'

'Mem—mem-ji—how can I thank you?' He bent to touch her feet again.

Nani smiled. 'Thank me by keeping my granddaughter safe.' Chandra beamed. 'Here is fifty rupees. My cook should have something ready for you by now, take it, and then go and fetch your family.'

Amrita, coming out of the kitchen with a sour face, broke into Bhawar's promises of loyalty as he bowed himself out. 'Mother-in-law, I'll not have her stay here. I won't have it, I say! Not with my four boys, I won't have them at risk. She'll bring trouble, kidnappers, violence—nahi, I'll not have it, and Raj will agree with me!' Her voice rose in defiance.

Nani and Chandra both regarded her with dislike and dismay. 'Agree with you?' nani eventually said gently. 'When you are so generous, considerate, and charming, how could my lucky son do anything else?'

Amrita's face flamed. 'Well, it's true! I'm not having my sons and myself in danger! Not for a wild-wilful girl who can't do as she should!'

'Ah?' Nani's tone was sweetly acid. 'You mean by obeying her mother-in-law without any argument, daughter-in-law?'

'Oh!' Amrita flounced off to her own room in a fury.

Nani looked at Chandra's pale face, and hugged her hard. 'Don't look so white-fright, my dear!'

'Do I have to go away again, nani?' Chandra whispered. 'I thought when I reached you, I'd be safe.'

'And so you will be, Chandra.' Nani was furious too, but resigned. 'That thorn-tongued scorpion! Even if I could persuade Raj to let you stay, the atmosphere would be like having a spitting cobra in the house. My poor son would be driven out of his feeble mind. And she seemed so mild-kind, when we inspected her . . . Ah, well. You can't be guarded all the rest of your life, anyway. Nahi, you can't stay here. We'll have to find somewhere else for you.'

'Have I caused trouble for you, nani? With her? By coming here?'

Her grandmother snorted. 'I have three other sons, and if she annoys me too much, I invite one of them to stay, with his family, and she has to attend to all of us—and she's terrified I leave my money to one of the others, so she can't be too disagreeable! Nahi, that's nothing for you to fret about, Chandra. It adds a bit of spice to life . . . But it would be really too nasty-noisy, to insist that you stay.' She shrugged. 'Oh, well. Let's go and lie down for the afternoon rest, child. And this evening, we'll find a secure place for you.'

Chandra rose wearily. During all the planning on the farm, all the way across the desert, all the time on the train, her dream had been of security with nani. But it wasn't that simple.

CHAPTER 11

The Mukherjees

Chandra couldn't rest. She tossed on the six-foot-wide bed in the guest room, uncomfortable on the soft mattress. The ceiling fan made her too cold. She finally switched it off, and lay down on the floor as usual, but still couldn't find peace. She peered through the shutters at the street traders wandering below; the key mender, the woman selling stainless steel bowls and plates, the man begging empty tins—sure sign of a rich colony—the gypsies playing and singing, hoping for a few paise tossed down. She examined the trinkets in the display case in the corner, fidgeted and fretted. But when eventually everyone stirred again, she had a suggestion for her grandmother. 'Nani, my best friends, Sangeeta or Urvashi, one of them'll take me in!'

'Accha! What a good idea!' Nani applauded her. 'And they're not so far away that Bhawar can't live here, and still look after you. So, which one is more progressive?'

Chandra made a face. 'Urvashi's mother is the only one I've met. She's marvellous, so . . . so motherly! She's huge, and her husband is so small—like an elephant and a monkey! Ai-ai, I'm sorry, I shouldn't joke like that! But I've only seen her father once, at a school prizegiving. Vashi whispered to me, and afterwards he scolded her for being unmannerly. He seems stickly-prickly, maybe? And she is very proper. Sangeeta always talks about being modern. Try her father first, nani.'

However, that evening when they telephoned Sangeeta's father, he flatly refused. 'My family to be implicated in a scam? Nahi, nahi.'

'Scam? A scam is illegal.' Nani's tone was sharp. 'You are saying that saving a girl from widow slavery is wrong?'

'Of course not, mem. But this is a matter for the police. I cannot help. Nahi, nahi.' His voice suddenly turned oily. 'Unless you wish me to act for you? You know I am a lawyer, my fees are very low-moderate, and for a friend of my daughter . . . Nahi?' His tone stiffened again. 'Then I cannot allow my child to be involved.'

He put the phone down just in time to miss nani's scathing, 'Coward and hypocrite! I hope you get boils on your backside! Don't worry, my dear,' she soothed Chandra. 'What was your other friend's name? Urvashi Mukherjee?'

To Chandra's surprise and relief Mr Mukherjee agreed instantly. 'Of course she may come, mem. I support tradition, as all men should, but not to extremes. I do pooja, I worship Krishna-Radha, I make gifts to the temple. OK, but I'm progressive as well. When I'm sick, I call a doctor for medicine, not a priest for a charm. I'll be glad to take Chandra in, mem.'

Nani and Chandra clasped hands thankfully.

When Chandra and Bhawar climbed out of the taxi at Urvashi's house they were surrounded by a flood of smiling youngsters, crying, 'Namaste! Namaste!' Urvashi pushed through them. 'Chandra, how good to see you again! Come along, mata and bapa are waiting for you. You remember my brothers and sisters? Of course you do, it's only three months—but you've changed so much, you're so skinny-scraggy! Ai, what a terrible thing, I said you were too young—hai, I'm so excited, I'm talking as much as Sangeeta!'

Happy at being freshly shaved and washed again after the dirt and grit of the train journey, and better dressed than he'd ever been in an old shirt and trousers of her husband's that Amrita had tossed at him—'I'll not have him going about our garage raggy-tatty and filthy as a Sadhu holy man, what would the neighbours say?'—Bhawar followed them up the stair with Chandra's small bag. He was nervous, but not as bad as he'd been at the old mem's house; he had a job and a home, he was on his way up!

'Namaste, child! I'm so happy to see you again! Nahi, nahi, don't bow to me!' Mrs Mukherjee enfolded Chandra in her comfortable arms. 'Call me Aunt Sita, if you can stand all these noisy funny-bunnies as your cousins!' The children all laughed happily. 'This shrimp is my husband, Sunil. I don't think you've met him, whenever you've been here he's always been at the factory, doing overtime.' She winked. 'He says! He has a pretty-witty secretary!'

The slight, small man half-hidden behind her expansive flower-patterned sari tickled her on the folds of her bare midriff, and she jumped aside, scolding him, 'Hai, Eve-teaser! Keep your hands to yourself!'

He smiled up at Chandra. 'I'm glad to meet you, Chandra. I've seen you before, but as my big she-elephant says—' he ducked in comical exaggeration as his wife slapped at him, and the room filled with the children's laughter again '—when I'm not aching-creaking from the beatings she gives me, I have to spend so much time making money for her to waste—'

'Waste! Who do I spend it on, eh?'

'—We've never actually met. You are welcome.' Why had she thought him stiff and very formal? He was calm, certainly, even while joking with his family. Somehow, in spite of his small size and his wife's vastness, he gave the impression of an elephant surrounded by puppies. But there was a twinkle in his eye. 'Your nani was too tired to come with you? A pity. A great lady! A memsahib!'

He looked past her to where Bhawar hesitated by the door. 'Your bodyguard—Bhawar, is it? Ha, this is like a gangster movie!' He shook his head. 'I don't know what you can do, really.' He considered Bhawar thoughtfully. 'You don't look like a fighting man.'

Bhawar spread his hands in a shrug. 'Nahi, sahib. But for the miss, I'll do anything. At least I can shout loudly!' They

81

all laughed. 'And if I am sitting on the stair, it will keep all robbers away from your home.'

'We've never had robbers,' Sunil said drily. 'But if they find out where she is, I suppose they might try just walking up and knocking on the door, hoping to find her alone. OK, Bhawar. Come in with the maid in the mornings, at eight, and you can go when I get in at eight at night. And be careful you're not followed here. OK?' Bhawar nodded eagerly. 'Have you no shoes?'

Bhawar gazed down at his worn plastic flip-flops. 'Nahi, sahib. I am ashamed to come into your beautiful house like this—'

'Never mind. Just get shoes this evening.' Sita reached for her purse. 'Here. Off you go, then—and be sure you come back tomorrow!'

'On my children's lives, mem!' Bhawar bowed himself out, beaming. Only twelve hours a day, sitting about, for thirty rupees, and gifts of new clothes and nearly a hundred rupees already! On his first day in Delhi! More than he'd ever made in two weeks! He'd make an offering to Ganesha for inspiring him to leave the farm and bringing him to where he could gain such fabulous wealth.

Aunt Sita hugged Chandra again. 'You've eaten? But you have room for a small bite-bit? There's not a mouthful for an ant on her, husband, we must feed her up. Vashi, take her to the girls' room, settle her in while I get us some titbits. Go on, child.'

Breathless under their welcome and concern, and the warmth and laughter in the house, Chandra smiled and relaxed. But that night, and for many nights, she had nightmares. 'Nahi—bapa—father-in-law . . . let me go! Help!' She couldn't make herself waken. She moaned and thrashed about in the big bed she shared with Urvashi and her two little sisters till Urvashi shook her awake, got her a cup of water, and soothed her. 'Calm, be calm, Chandra! You're safe! No one can get at you here in our house!'

It was a lovely house, not as large as nani's but more modern, clean and airy, with yellow painted walls and polished marble-chip floors, on the top floor of a five-storey block. As well as the kitchen and washroom—there was a sit-down European toilet beside the proper Indian one; how disgustingly dirty, to put your skin down where someone else's had been just a short time before, and to wipe yourself with paper instead of washing! Chandra avoided even looking at it—there were four rooms, one for the girls and one for the boys, their parents' room and the living-room. If a child was particularly noisy, Uncle Sunil threatened to stuff him into the huge fridge in the big kitchen; he was so rich, he didn't need to show it off in the living-room.

On the flat roof above, Aunt Sita grew big pots of chrysanthemums and jasmine round a little trellis arbour shading a swing and a big cage with singing birds. It was peaceful, with the roar and dust of traffic lost below and the kite-hawks soaring above. Chandra went out only in the evening, with the whole family round her; as Aunt Sita said, 'Snails are safer than butterflies!' During the day, while the children were out at school or nursery school, the maid and cook were busy in the flat, and Bhawar dozed happily on the stair, she spent a lot of time up on the roof, talking to the birds and relaxing on the airy swing, recovering slowly, flying a paper kite, playing computer games, praying, reading, or just sitting looking out over the trees and rooftops to the gleaming pink domes of the Shiva temple, thinking.

Sunil Mukherjee was manager of a factory that made high-quality casings for electrical equipment like computers. Chandra liked and respected the competent little man very much, and was glad he approved of what she had done. 'Ai, your father's family are real old fogeys. Rigid conservatives. But things change. You know in the early traditions women were the equal of men?'

'What? "Woman is as foul as falsehood itself", bapa always said.'

'Ji haa, the teachings of Manu.' Uncle Sunil chuckled. 'A psychologist would say his mother maybe smacked him too much.' A mother, smacking a son? Sunil laughed aloud at Chandra's appalled face. 'But at other times even he said that men should protect and respect women. Anyway, that was about the time of Jesus Christ, two thousand years ago, niece. The world changes. And purdah, keeping women indoors out of the sight of men, only started at the time of the Mogul invasions four hundred years ago, when we had to keep our wives and daughters hidden from the Muslims. Or some say that it's to help men control women.' His eyebrows wriggled, as they did whenever he made a joke. 'All men are afraid of women's power—ask Sita!'

Chandra made herself smile politely. This was all topsy-turvy. Bapa said women must fear and obey men. But Durga had saved the world by destroying a dreadful demon when the gods had failed. Men afraid of women? A new idea . . .

Sunil was nodding. 'But the world changes. Respect for women, as people, not as possessions, is growing. Many teachers have spoken for women's rights—Ram Mohan, Tilak, Vivekananda—oh, many many. I'll get you a book of their teachings. And we have great women in our past as well as our present. Lakshmi Bai—'

Chandra nodded eagerly. 'I prayed to her for courage when I was afraid in Jaisalmer.'

'Good for you! And Indira Ghandi was Prime Minister here, and Benazir Bhutto in Pakistan. They've shown women are mentally as good as men.' His eyebrows twitched. 'Or as bad!'

'What?' It surprised Chandra that he showed no anger or jealousy. 'Bapa always said that it proved they weren't true women.'

Sunil smiled, his head quizzically to one side. 'You really are a good, loyal beti, Chandra. But trust can go too far. After all you've been through, you still think your bapa is always right?'

Bapa not always right? Guilty at her disloyalty and disobedience, she'd always refused to admit the thought. It was almost painful, after so many years of strict training. To actually hear it suggested was terrifying. But . . .

The world changed. She gritted her teeth, and nodded. Ji haa. It was true. So say it . . . say it . . . Bapa could be wrong!

And if so, then maybe she wasn't so bad, to disobey him?

CHAPTER 12

The Price of Freedom

Aunt Sita was a tutor midwife in the East-West Nursing Centre. While she was out at work, and the children at school or nursery, Chandra often watched the television. The maid and the cook were delighted; they weren't allowed to touch the set, or sit in the armchairs, but when she switched on, as soon as their work was done they squatted with Bhawar in the doorway to watch. Chandra found every programme interesting, whether it was on make-up, politics, or music, and the English language ones helped her English revive. But they all loved films best. They cheered the heroes, sang and danced with the songs, hissed the villains, and thoroughly enjoyed them-selves—though Chandra had to admit that bapa was right about this at least; films really were a bad example. In the European ones, there was even kissing!

Chandra didn't dare go back to school, but she helped Urvashi and the younger ones with their homework. After they'd finished, the children were allowed to watch television too, and Chandra's status in the household shot up when they found that she could translate the English language programmes for them. She didn't tell them how much of the dialogue she invented—though she sometimes saw Mr Mukherjee bite his lips to hide a grin.

She particularly enjoyed the serialized epic of the *Mahabharata*, admiring the great heroes and lovely ladies in their glittering costumes. 'Ah, look at the crowns and jewels! Gorgeous!' she sighed one day.

Little Munir, only four, was sitting on her knee to watch. He twisted round to see her face, and started to chortle. 'They're not real, cousin! It's just make-believe gold and glass. Listen, everybody!' He yelled the joke to the rest. 'Chandra thinks it's all real gold!'

They fell about the floor, laughing. Chandra blushed. Urvashi gently scolded Munir, 'These are jungly manners, little brother, embarrassing a guest. What would your Miss at the Little Buds Nursery School say?'

But Chandra hugged to herself the secret of her own jewels, real gold and rubies, safe in her drawer upstairs. It was wonderful to know that something of hers was better than anything on the marvellous TV!

In February, after Chandra had lazed about for a full month, putting on some weight so that Aunt Sita no longer tutted about how bony she was, nani arrived unexpectedly one evening. 'Namaste, nani-ji! I didn't expect you till Friday as usual.' Chandra's face brightened in hope. 'Have you heard from mata?'

Nani shook her head. 'Not yet, my dear. Your father won't allow her to go out at all, or write, I'm afraid.' She had visited her daughter when she knew Vijay would be out, but when she panted up the dark, dirty stair to knock and call, she heard only sobs, and Varahi's voice calling, 'Nahi, nahi! I am a good wife, I obey my husband, I will not speak to you, I have no beti! Go away! Mata, please, please go away!' She'd not tell Chandra that.

'Oh, dear.' Chandra's shoulders slumped.

Nani snorted briskly. 'Don't be so helpless! You are Chandra! You can manage without them!'

Chandra longed for the close warmth of her family again . . . nervous, loving mata, tetchy bapa, Kirpal and Deepak bullying her in a friendly way as older brothers always did . . . But of course she could manage without them!

She'd have to.

At least she still had nani, and Urvashi, Aunt Sita, Uncle Sunil, the children here. She wasn't all alone. She tried to cheer up. 'Why are you here, then, nani—and looking so birdy-chirpy?'

'Aha! Wait and see!' Maddeningly, nani took time to give Aunt Sita a box of sweets, thank her and Sunil for their care and kindness, settle fussily in a high-backed cane chair, take a glass of mango juice from Urvashi, smooth her sari neatly while Chandra fidgeted. But at last she stopped teasing and told her news. 'I've found a home for you, my dear!'

'Nani-ji! Oh, thank Durga! And thank you!' Chandra and Urvashi, side by side on the settee, clapped their hands.

'I had to! Men have been watching my house!' She nodded confirmation to their shocked gasps. 'Ji haa! Your father-in-law must have sent them. I got the watchman to chase one away, but next day there was another one. I told Bhawar to be very careful about coming here, and I checked myself to see that my taxi wasn't followed!' She chuckled, her dark, lively old eyes bright in their fine net of wrinkles. 'It's like a film thriller! So exciting! Such an adventure, at my age!'

'But what have you planned, nani-ji?'

'Aha!' Her grandmother sobered herself. 'My telephone is glowing red-hot, and the bill will be lakhs of rupees! You remember your Aunt Manju? You last saw her when you were three.'

'I think so. The one who married an Englishman?'

'A Scottishman, she says—he is very strict about that! It seems to be like calling a Brahmin an untouchable.' She rolled her eyes in fake horror, as they all laughed. 'She lives in a small town called Glasgow. Only about half a million people. She says it's beautiful countryside round about, but chilly-cold, even in summer, like Kashmir.'

Smiling, she explained to the Mukherjees, 'Manju went to study special midwife nursing in England. She met a young teacher, who asked her to marry him. And she agreed. And we had never even met him!'

'Oh, dear!' Aunt Sita shook her head in sympathy. 'Children nowadays, always wanting to choose for themselves—as if their parents had not far more experience, to know who will be suitable!' She looked over at Sunil. 'We've been happy, eh? And we only met once before the wedding.'

He smiled at her. 'But we could both have refused, if we'd disliked each other too much. And even before I agreed to meet you, I arranged to get a look at you first, when you were visiting one of my aunts!' He smiled again, expecting her to be astonished, and looked amazed when she just smirked. 'You knew? Oh, you shameless gypsy!'

She laughed aloud. 'Why do you think I was in my best sari that day, eh? Of course I knew you'd be there.' Her eyes sparkled with fun and challenge. 'I saw you, too—in a mirror, while you were chatting to your uncle. Or I'd not have met you, either.'

'You wicked—oh, you demon! Wait till we're alone!' Sunil threatened her. Shaking a fist at her, he turned back to nani. 'My apologies, mem. It must have been terrible for you, when your daughter told you.'

Nani was smiling too, but she nodded sideways in agreement. 'Ji haa. But she was always a rebellious one. And she'd already broken caste. And at least she met his parents, and they liked her.' Everyone nodded in approval; at least some traditions had been observed. Nani lifted her hands in a shrug. 'They agreed she could stay in her own religion, he would fit in with our diet. And then she was hit by a car. She can have no children.'

'Ah, what a tragedy!' Aunt Sita, happily surrounded by her own well-loved brood, was appalled. 'Did he not break off the engagement?'

'Nahi. He still wanted to wed her in spite of it. He must be a good man, even if he is white. No Indian man would have married her, so . . . ' Nani shrugged again. 'We agreed—what else could we do? Anyway, she's very happy, she says, apart from this one sorrow. Because they're of different races, it's somehow impossible for them to adopt a baby. I offered to buy one for them from a poor good-caste family here, but they said that wouldn't be allowed either. So strange! And working all day with babies, it is hard, hard for her. So, Chandra, they'll adopt you.'

Chandra had already realized what nani was going to say. Her mouth was open in shock. England! Oh, Durga!

Chuckling at her astonishment, nani went on, 'That should be allowed, since you are family already. And if not, you'll just stay with them anyway.'

Thrilled, Chandra and Urvashi gripped hands so tight it hurt, and exchanged delighted grins. Going to England! Marvellous!

Sunil, however, looked doubtful. 'How will you get her to England, mem? It takes a long time to get a permit. My cousin took two years. And what about a passport? Her bapa would need to sign for her to get it, and will he?'

Nani waved her finger triumphantly. 'That's all taken care of! A friend of my son Raj often goes to England. He is going in three days, and his daughter was going with him, to meet a nice young man in Manchester, but she's fallen ill. Mumps!' They all made sounds of commiseration, but they couldn't help smiling. 'Ah, how sad, poor girl—and how funny! And how perfect for us! For no husband would take her, the way she looks just now, all lumpy-bumpy, and her father was moaning to Raj that he doubted if he'd get a full refund on the girl's ticket, it was so near the date for the flight, and for once Raj had a good idea all on his own. He suggested that instead, his friend could take you, Chandra! Smuggle you in!'

They all considered it for a minute. 'What if she's caught?' Urvashi asked. 'What would they do?'

Nani shrugged. 'What can they do, to a child? Send her back? She'll be no worse off than now.' She patted Chandra's arm. 'But they'll not notice you. Europeans are blind; they themselves admit they can't tell Indians apart.'

The first glow of excitement was fading a little, and Chandra was starting to feel . . . not exactly scared, but awed by the size of the idea. 'It's a long, long way, nani. Is there no one closer I could go to?'

Nani was resigned. 'No one. I really-truly have tried everyone! My other children and my nieces are ill, or have no room. Your father will tell your father-in-law about them, anyway. I don't want to risk bringing trouble on them. And all my good friends are dead, years ago.' She reached over to pat Chandra's hand. 'Don't worry, you'll manage beautifully!'

'You always topped in English, Chandra!' Urvashi was encouraging. 'England! I wish it was me! I hope you'll invite me to stay, some day!'

Gratefully, Chandra nodded. 'Of course! Any time!'

'Hush, beti! Think about it seriously. This is a terrible thing, mem. She'd lose caste, going across the ocean, living outside proper society, especially with a lady who is—unconventional, and a white man,' Aunt Sita mused, puffing out her plump cheeks. 'Isn't that important to you, mem?'

'Not as important as keeping her safe.' Nani was determined. 'It's not what I would choose if there was any other way, but I can find nothing. Nothing! I hate to lose her, but the gods send our path. And it's not for ever. She can be cleansed when she returns. It's common enough, anyway, nobody makes a fuss-buzz about it. Raj's friend does it often.'

'It's a great risk for him,' Uncle Sunil said doubtfully. 'Why would he—ah! You're paying him?'

Nani clapped her hands in resignation. 'That is the problem. He will do it, but his price is sky-high. He says he won't risk years in jail, and the loss of his trading permits, and so of his business, if he's caught, for a handful of rice. He wants a dowry for his daughter.'

'Aha!' Sunil nodded thoughtfully. 'How much?'

'A lakh of rupees.'

Chandra's jaw dropped. Sunil whistled. 'A hundred thousand! So much, to smuggle her in? I thought ten thousand—'

'Ji haa, for a ride nailed up in a crate in the back of a lorry, robbed or dumped on the street in Belgium, or even sold to a Muslim slaver! Nahi.' Nani was firm. 'The price is high, but it includes her ticket, passport, a respectable man to accompany her till she meets Manju—everything. And she goes now, when she needs to go.'

'You can't afford so much, nani!' Chandra protested.

Nani nodded. 'No, you're right. I can't. But don't despair. It's more than I can pay, but not more than can be paid.' They all stared at her in puzzlement. She took Chandra's hand between her old wrinkled ones. 'Chandra, my dear. You have the price of your own safety. Will you give up your jewellery to buy your journey to England?'

Chandra felt as if her heart was freezing. She could feel her face, usually smiling, was now twisting with tension. She knew they were all watching her anxiously, wanting to help—but it had to be her choice. She wished they weren't there . . . but no, she was glad of the warm support of their love through the shuddering chill of this ordeal. She tugged her hands away from her grandmother's clasp, rubbing her tight-clenched fists against each other in anguish.

Her gold and rubies, her own, only treasure! Nahi! Never!

But if her father-in-law was following nani . . . He'd find her, and drag her back to Jaisalmer somehow, unlawful or not . . . Where in India would she be safe?

Everything has to be paid for—and maybe not in rupees.

But her lovely necklace? The bangles and ear-rings, the pendant . . . ?

Ah, how silly! She'd lose them anyway, if she was taken back. She banged her fists on her knees. Any sacrifice was better than that!

She heaved a long breath, the first, it seemed, for years, and nodded shakily. 'Ji haa, nani. If I have to. Ji haa. OK.'

She burst into tears. 'Ai-ai, I hate them!' Urvashi put an arm round her waist and started to cry in sympathy.

Aunt Sita rose hastily. 'I'll get us something to eat.' Food always cheered people up.

Two nights later the festival of Shivaratri celebrated the tandava, the dance of enlightenment, when Shiva, angered by the opposition of ten thousand holy men, danced in a ring of fire to display to them his power as the moving force of the universe, creating it, preserving it, embodying it, and finally at the end of time destroying it and releasing souls from illusion. Some day, if he was dissatisfied with the worship given him, he would dance the dance of destruction . . . Temple bells rang all night, and the sacred lingams in Shiva temples and shrines all over India were flooded with milk and perfume.

Chandra watched and fasted all day with the Mukher- jees, but when they went to make their temple offerings, she stayed behind. On the roof under the stars, bright in the moonless night, she prayed alone. 'Durga, great goddess, power of women; Shiva, world-destroyer and creator; I make pooja to you, I prostrate myself before you. Don't destroy me. Great ones, preserve me, even me, Chandra, the smallest of people. Help me, keep me safe, even far away across the black waters. Remember me, please; I am Chandra.'

A gong sounded, deep and soft, far off on her right side, the lucky side. A breeze gently cooled her forehead, like the breath of a god. She knew she was answered.

CHAPTER 13

The Market

'England is chilling-freezing, all the time, niece.' In a frantic rush before Chandra left, Aunt Sita insisted on buying her woollen underwear, a thick cardigan from Kashmir, a red anorak, heavy tights to go under her new sneakers, and a red knitted set of scarf, gloves, and a hat with a blue pom-pom, from Darjeeling. She called in a tailor to take Chandra's measurements for a warm kameez and salwar suit, in blue wool with red piping, to be made within twenty-four hours. 'That's better! Now you should be hot as a little chilli!'

When Chandra murmured that she felt overwhelmed by this generosity, Urvashi argued, 'She's just like that, Chandra. She enjoys giving-helping. And the guest is god, to care for you earns merit to help her in the next life, if there is one. Really-truly you owe her nothing. To make a big thing of it would insult her. Please leave it!'

'Nahi, nahi! I've got to do something for her in return,' Chandra protested. 'I can't just take-grab, like a beggar! Could I get her a present? Let's see. I've got twenty-seven rupees left. That's not a lot. What could I get for that?'

'I know!' Urvashi looked pleased. 'If you feel you must get her something, I know just what she wants, she was saying only yesterday. A loose-leaf folder to clip in recipes from magazines. A nice pink one. They're about twenty-five rupees, in the market round the corner.'

'Accha! Perfect! Come on,' Chandra suggested, 'let's get it now before you start your homework.' Urvashi hesitated. 'Ah, Vashi, I'm tired of being in the house all day. Come on! You'll be there, and we'll have Bhawar with us. It's time he did something to earn his money, instead of just sitting out on the landing getting flabby-fat!'

'But . . .' Urvashi still looked rather doubtful. Then she shrugged. 'Oh, well, why not? Mata's busy making sweets. The market's only a hundred yards away, we'll be back before anyone notices we've gone.'

Bhawar's mat outside was empty. Urvashi looked annoyed. 'I remember now, mata asked him to go for some okra and cauliflower. We shouldn't—'

'Oh, never mind!' Chandra urged her. 'Cauliflower? He'll be at the market, won't he? We can meet him there. Come on, Vashi, who's to know I'm here? Bhawar's sure he hasn't been followed. And I feel like a chicken in a coop. If I don't stretch my legs they'll drop off!'

Little Munir came out of the boys' room. 'Where are you going?' he demanded, peering inquisitively at the open door.

'Out to the market, just for a minute,' his big sister told him. She glanced after Chandra, already cheerfully jumping down the stairs. Better be sure . . . 'If we're not back soon, tell mata where we are. OK?'

'OK!' He was already half-way into the kitchen. Mmm, the smell of sugared lentils cooking for dal barfis! He always helped mata make them; he could eat lots before he felt sick . . .

Walking down the street chattering happily, the girls didn't notice a tall man squatting at the corner stall, chewing thoughtfully at a pan leaf. But he noticed them. Yes, that was the slut, her father had guessed right about where she was staying. Someone had lent her a blue sari. Her hair was cut like a convict's in a disgraceful short western style just as her father had said, her face shamelessly uncovered to be seen by any stranger. The other one was smaller, in a green school uniform; nothing to fear there. Ashish, Chandra's brother-in-law, spat out a squirt of red pan juice, whistled

95

to wake his brother dozing in a taxi down the street, and moved quietly after the girls.

The second man called the taxi driver from where he was squatting chatting to his friends, and pointed. 'Follow him. Not too close.'

'Like a film, eh, sahib? Follow that car!' Chuckling, the driver started up.

'Here it is.' Urvashi turned aside between two blocks into a short lane lined with small stalls selling sweets and ice cream, salted nuts, cigarettes, cold drinks. Fifty feet along, it opened into a big triangular space among the high blocks, packed with rainbow colour and gentle bustle.

Chandra gazed round in delight. 'You know, Vashi, this was what I missed most in Rajasthan. Going out to market. And school, of course, but the scents here—smell those spices! And the noise—listen, that's Lata Mangeshkar singing, isn't it? I wish I had enough money for a cassette.' She sighed. 'Do you think they have markets like this in England?'

'I don't know.' Urvashi shrugged. 'I've never seen one on the films. They're all rich-rich, maybe they don't go to market. Maybe they send their servants to do the buying for them.'

'They don't have servants, they have machines instead.' Chandra frowned. 'I think so, anyway.' She made a face. 'Oh, well, come on, let's have a good look round while we're here. I may never see it again, you know.' That was a frightening thought.

Stalls lined all three sides, draped and piled high with goods of a hundred kinds: T-shirts, gaudy posters of gods and film stars and kittens, folding chairs in wood and aluminium, sandals, locks, sari cloths, detergents, metal cups, knitting wool, cassettes, spectacles, radios, suitcases, bras, bags, bronze statuettes carefully greened to look antique.

In the shadiest corner was the food market. Under the shelter of striped awnings the girls admired the brilliant, multi-coloured vegetables and fruits, from black aubergines and golden cobs of corn to green mangoes and purple star-apples. There wasn't much interesting about ramparts of potatoes or the sacks of rice, wheat, sesame, barley, a dozen seeds, but here and there bright trays heaped high with spices and powdered dyes glowed in the dim light.

On one stall metal trays were slithery with silver, blue, and red fish on melting ice; in an open space four openwork baskets like deflating wicker footballs two metres wide and forty centimetres high, stuffed with unhappily clucking white chickens, surrounded the chopping block with its big fixed knife for preparing them. Skinny dogs snapped up the chicken skins and guts. Big, placid cream and black cows strolled about, hoovering up the vegetable rubbish: banana and orange skins, outside leaves of cauliflowers and cabbages, old cardboard boxes finally so broken as to be unusable again.

The far corner was stacked high with terracotta pots of all sizes, from palm-wide saucers for festival oil lamps to huge water-jars over a metre tall, and beside them, gaudy painted statues of gods and goddesses. 'You should take a Ganesha with you for luck, Chandra.' Urvashi looked up at one statue, two metres tall, in brilliant pink; 'Will this go in your hand luggage?' They didn't go further; in the lane beyond there sprawled only the junk merchants' piles of paper, bottles, oilcans, bicycle and car parts.

In the centre, on cloths spread on the ground in the baking sun, umbrellas and tattered cloths on bamboo sticks shaded poorer merchants crouching to display their wares. Beside his last the cobbler had sole-sized pieces of car tyre to cut to shape. The false-teeth man displayed his tin moulds and racks of teeth, ready to fit you while you waited. A boy sat by a handcart filled with computer and radio parts. The girls examined tangled piles of glittering plastic bangles, toys, shoes, combs, pretty stick-on tilaks for the forehead, long tassels of red or black thread to weave into the hair, old clothes, soap, and bleach. Urvashi paid ten rupees for a lipstick. 'Don't tell mata!'

Among drifts of dark hair trimmings, a barber shaved an old man with a flashing cut-throat razor. He grinned up at the girls. 'Faster than lightning, smooth as a baby's bottom, make him handsome and young again!' he boasted.

'A miracle! A miracle!' The old man's wife, squatting beside them, cackled in glee, while the spectators laughed and applauded.

The girls picked their way among the bright saris and shirts, among roaming beggars, dogs, bicycles; a ponderous ox-cart delivering sacks of rice; boys offering bidis, hand-rolled cigarettes, at two for a rupee; a water-seller with a big brass can slung on his back and six metal cups clinking on strings round his neck; a few fidgety, wall-eyed goats; an old auto-rickshaw van glinting with tinsel tassels; a smart new pony ekka, with green fringes on its hood; two little girls, untouchables with dark skins and wide faces, in torn pink satin party frocks, balancing hub-caps on their heads as dishes to collect cowdung for their grandmother in a far corner to knead into fuel cakes; a row of cycle rickshaws waiting for customers; and a man with a tall staff festooned with gorgeous balloons, some shaped like huge apples, some twisted into fantastic rattles for children.

Behind them, Bhawar left the shade of a vegetable stall in a hurry. He'd discovered that the stall-keeper came from a village only fifty miles from his own home, and they'd been chatting for too long. The sea-green of Urvashi's school uniform caught his eye, and then Chandra's short hair. Little brother wasn't supposed to be out without him! But he was here, at least. And this was his excuse for being slow; he'd been doing his main job, looking after the miss. He relaxed. His eye was caught by a small blue and yellow checked shirt on a stall. His eldest son Ram would like that . . .

'Is that the bookstall with the folders?' Chandra edged through the throng up to the counter, eyeing the cards of ball-points and pencils, the birthday and festival cards and writing paper, the new and second-hand books.

'Look, an *Asterix* book in Hindi. I love him, don't you? Hai, there's *David Copperfield*, that's stolen from our school, there's the stamp!' Urvashi's thick eyebrows rose accusingly towards the stallkeeper. 'You must take it back!' He spread his hands in a rueful shrug, and nodded sideways to agree. He wouldn't, of course.

'What's that one? Japanese flower arranging? Accha, how practical!' Chandra chuckled. Casually, she lifted a folder. The stall-holder beamed, not fooled at all by her pretence of indifference. 'How much are these? Forty rupees? Nahi, far too much. Fifteen. Besides, I want a red one, and you only have pink and green.' Chaffering happily, she paid no attention to two men standing nearby. 'Thirty? Still too much. Twenty, maybe, for a red one. Twenty-two for this pink one? No bent corners? Accha, OK.' As it was slipped into a neat newspaper envelope for her, she beamed at Urvashi, and then sighed. 'Ai, ai, that's that. I suppose we'd better go back now?'

Behind them, Bhawar had bought the little shirt; the boy would like it—ha, the misses were leaving! 'Hurry up, woman, I can't wait here till the rains come!'

The stallkeeper snorted, deftly wrapping his purchase in a page of a magazine. 'OK, maharajah! What's wrong? Your wife and your girl-friend both come into the market?' The women sitting round her screamed with laughter.

Half-way down the lane Chandra paused. 'Wait a moment, Vashi, I've got five rupees left, I'll get some spiced noodles for Munir—'

A cloth flew over her head. An arm pinned her arms to her sides, and a hand clamped across her mouth. Strong hands gripped her knees, lifted, and she was swept off her feet and carried forward.

Rigid with terror, she knew what was happening. They were taking her back. Her nightmare was upon her. And this time she couldn't wake up . . .

Durga! Durga, great goddess, help me! Help me!

CHAPTER 14

Riot

Great goddess, help me . . . Durga . . .

Chandra's mind fell and fell, into a blank, endless space. Sounds echoed eerily, slowly, round the black rim of her skull. Her staring eyes could see nothing in the emptiness . . . Except a form, blacker against black. A face, screaming in frenzied rage, mouth and tongue smeared with blood. Four arms, brandishing weapons. A necklace of heads, a girdle of severed arms. Eyes, red as blood, rolling drunkenly . . .

Kali. Kali Mata. The Black Mother, the terrifying form of Durga, the crazy fighter who had destroyed the giant with a thousand arms, and then torn her husband Shiva to pieces in her killing madness . . .

A huge voice boomed slowly, like a vast gong in her head. CHANDRA, MY BETI, UNDER MY PROTECTIONNN, CHAAANDRAAAA . . . DESTROYYYTHEMMMM . . .

No, not destroy, too bad, too much . . . No, please . . .

DESTROYYY . . .

No . . .

Invincible power flowed into her, her skin filled to bursting with energy, her muscles were lightning, her blood was fire . . . She jack-knifed, fast, and straightened out as hard as she could. Her head slammed stunningly into a jawbone above her. The rough grip slipped, one foot came free; she kicked, and connected. A satisfying squawk of pain. A finger slid into her mouth; she bit down on it, and felt a bone crack between her teeth. The man yelled, tugged his hand away, she let go before she lost a tooth and used her mouth for screaming, 'Help! Kidnap! Murder! Help!' as she landed in the dust.

Urvashi had been pushed so hard she landed on her hands and knees. Stumbling up, shaken, she saw two men carrying Chandra off towards a taxi. She grabbed the folder up from the pavement as she rose, and flailed it uselessly at the men, screeching, 'Help! Help!'

At the same moment, Bhawar reached them, yelling to waken his courage. It was really happening, he'd have to actually, physically hit somebody. Oh, Rama, he'd never fought anybody since he left school! But something drove him on—must save her . . . Fists flailing wildly, he charged at the man staggering from Chandra's head-butt to his chin and knocked him over. Two men, maybe more—he couldn't beat two—a scene from a film flashed into his mind, and instantly he copied it. 'Muslims, carrying off a Hindu girl! Help! Muslims!'

The nearby stall-holders, those who had noticed anything at all in the five seconds of the attack, had been only concerned to keep the scuffle away from their goods, but that cry roused every Hindu to fury. Even one of the men who had seized Chandra shouted, 'Muslims? Where?'

Muffled in the cloth, dazed by the bump on her head, her ears full of the boom of Kali's voice, Chandra heard nothing of this. As she fell, she dragged the cloth off her head; she rolled aside, saw trouser legs around her, jumped to her feet and started running straight ahead, away from the men; away from the road, up the lane, back into the market. Her attackers chased her. Shouting, 'Muslims!' five stall-keepers ran after them. Bhawar yelled the Hindu battle-cry; 'Ram Ram!' The market stopped dead, leapt to its feet, looked for trouble; found it and joined in.

Behind Chandra as she ran, she could hear feet thudding close. Someone was gasping, 'Stop, miss, stop!' Stop? No fear! The goddess had given her strength and speed; she dodged lightly among the stalls. Her pursuers hit them, damaged them, roused more men into the chase. 'Ram Ram!' Eighty men now. Who was chasing whom?

Across the open centre. The balloon man's staff fell, and his stock exploded like gunfire under the pounding feet, and a stand of locks clattered down under the nose of the ekka pony. It reared and bolted, the shafts rattling on its skinny ribs, right across the market-place, women and children leaping in terror; a wheel of the little carriage caught against a letter-box, the axle broke, the ekka fell and smashed, and the pony galloped on down the lane, broken shards of wood and cloth trailing and banging its legs behind to spur it panicking onward into the main road.

'Ram Ram! Ram Ram!' Two hundred men.

Chandra swung round a post into the food market; the men behind collided with it, bringing down piles of baskets to bounce like footballs among their feet, trip them stumbling into trays of dyes and spices. Kicked high, the powders drifted in a choking rainbow riot over clothes and hair. Fruit stalls disintegrated, the bright displays tumbling and squishing to a mottled, muddy carpet.

The passionate, hysterical roar of the crowd grew higher, deeper, louder. 'Ram Ram! Ram Ram!' Screaming women seized their children and fled, men leaped to save their stock, or to attack the enemy—any enemy.

Chandra ran faster, dodging through the narrow passageways. *In the haze of dust above, Kali grinned at her, gave her strength, urged her on, spurred on the mob, her red tongue thirsty for blood.*

Two chemists' stalls crashed to the dust together, mingling fake western pills and Ayurvedic herbal cures. A tailor jumped aside as his sewing machine was knocked over, and he joined in the mob, yelling, 'Villains! Get them! Where are they? Find them! Ram Ram!'

The cry echoed from the tall flats and offices all round. Clerks and coolies raced out to join in. 'Ram Ram! Ram Ram!' Five hundred men running. As many leaning out of windows, cheering them on.

Four cows quietly chewing the cud in a corner, terrified by the noise, stampeded out on to the main road; the screech of lorry brakes, the crashing of metal went unheard in the din.

A three-year-old beggar child running for safety stopped to grab at a melon, her five-year-old brother paused to snatch her on, the crowd charged over both of them. Men and women tripped on the debris of stalls, fell and were lost underfoot, their screams lost equally among the roar.

'Ram Ram! Ram Ram!'

Suddenly the goddess abandoned Chandra. She stumbled over the corner of a broken stall, and landed on her knees. Blind feet knocked her flat, trampled over her. She'd be smashed, killed, pounded into the dust . . .

Her arm was twisting, breaking . . . Someone was dragging her off to the side, away from the mob. She was alive . . . They'd got her . . .

At least she was alive. Did it matter, then, if she was hauled back to slavery in Jaisalmer?

Yes! With the last of her energy, her own energy, she drove herself to her knees, turned clawing to defend herself from this man lifting her up, shoving her back—'Miss! Little brother! It's me, Bhawar! Stop! Don't hit me! You're safe now! It's Bhawar! I've saved you!'

It took a few seconds for the words to make sense. Where was she . . . ? Tucked tight in a corner beside a strong railing. Bhawar, half his new shirt purple with dye, blood pouring from a gash in his right arm, was holding the railing, shoving her back, his body protecting her from the torrent of people roaring past just beyond the angle where they pressed in, sheltered and safe.

Gasping, she stared round.

Behind the railing, a group of women were sobbing in the back door of a block of flats. There was no sign of her attackers. Or of Urvashi.

Red lights were flashing, sirens wailing to drown the women's crying. The police. White and khaki uniforms came charging through the mist of dyes and spices drifting among the raised dust, and long staves lashed out at

103

shoulders and feet to end the little riot. The roar of furious voices rose in tone, broke, faded away to shouting and moaning, shouts and moans.

Chandra stood panting, recovering her breath and her senses, Bhawar's arm round her shoulders for support. Oh, Durga! Kali! What a destruction! She hadn't wanted this! Don't ask the gods for help . . . Her knees collapsed under her. Bhawar lowered her gently to sit down in the dust. For some reason she looked at her watch; not fifteen minutes had passed since they'd left home.

Home . . . 'Urvashi. Look for Urvashi.' Her whisper was husky, her throat cracking dry. She didn't move. Couldn't move.

People were beginning to creep back, wailing, helping the injured, picking up the desolate fragments of their possessions. Bhawar pulled off his torn sleeve to tie round the gash in his arm. 'How did that happen?' he said. 'I can't remember much.' Neither could Chandra . . .

Just by her feet, a basket full of chickens had been trampled to a tatter of grey and pink feathers among a scatter of wicker twigs. A survivor clucked in a puzzled tone, standing on one leg on the side of the overturned auto-rickshaw. Its other leg was broken. At one side the cobbler's last, unbreakable, held down a strip of yellow chiffon floating on a waft of air like a pennant on top of a jagged pile of firewood and rags that was the remains of five stalls and two rickshaws.

Empty of feeling, still shocked, Chandra sat still, leaning against Bhawar's leg. She felt it trembling. 'Bhawar, why. . . ' Her voice trailed away.

A man appeared through the slowly-settling fog of dust, shirtless and filthy, one trouser leg ripped from the knee, half-carrying, half-dragging another. She knew him; Ashish. He stopped, and stared at her through a mask of red and green; some blood, some dye. Too exhausted to run, all the strength that the goddess had lent her gone, she stared back.

Bhawar steadied himself on the railings. Lord Rama, don't let him go for her, not again . . .

After a long ten seconds, Ashish hawked and spat. 'Some day . . . ' His voice was hoarse, his eyes bloodshot. 'We'll not forget you. Some day . . . ' He heaved up his hurt, or dead, partner, and limped away into the mist.

After a while, she managed to whisper, 'What now, Bhawar?'

He took a long minute to straighten his back stiffly. 'We take you home, little brother.'

'There she is.' A man's voice. Uncle Sunil, always reliable.

'Chandra? Chandra! Ai, thank the gods! Are you hurt?' Urvashi.

She was almost too weary to turn her head. 'Vashi, you're safe?'

Urvashi used an end of her dupatta to wipe Chandra's filthy face. 'You look . . . dreadful! Are you hurt?' she repeated.

Chandra shook her head, but as she tried to haul herself to her feet she gasped with pain from bruises she'd not realized she had. Sunil slid an arm round her and helped her up. 'Come along, niece. I'm glad you're still alive.'

'Only thanks to Bhawar.'

Sunil blinked. He'd been blaming Bhawar for going off, even if it was Sita who had sent him, and had been only holding himself in from berating him because he didn't want to upset Chandra further. Now he nodded acceptance, seeing Bhawar's weariness, the start of a huge black eye, and his shirt sleeve bandaging his arm. The man had been in the fighting, anyway. And if Chandra said he'd saved her . . . 'Accha, Bhawar. We'll leave explanations till we get back. Sita's crazy with worry.'

Slumping on to his arm, Chandra felt the weight of guilt. 'If I hadn't gone out—' Four men carried a stretcher past, with a child on it. 'Oh, dear!'

'Hush-hush! Let's go home.'

105

An hour later, washed and in fresh clothes, Bhawar stood proudly beside the door. His eye was swollen so that he could hardly see out of it, the gash in his arm was aching and stinging with antiseptic and stitching—it was handy that the mem was a nurse! But his heart was singing in triumph. He was a hero! The sahib had said so, while he was telephoning the old mem to let her know that her grandchild was still safe, in spite of the news on the radio.

All the Mukherjees sat round the big table in the living-room, solemn-faced and silent as Urvashi described what had happened. 'I jumped out in the road and stopped a police jeep, mata, and they radioed for help when we heard the war-cry.' She was rather proud of herself, too.

Chandra, in a new sari, confirmed it hoarsely. 'But it was Bhawar who saved me. He dragged me out of the way of the rampaging crowd. From under their feet. I was actually being trampled—and he could have been, too, if he'd slipped. He was very brave.'

Sunil looked up at the little man. 'We owe you a great deal, Bhawar.' Bhawar beamed. 'When Chandra leaves I'll give you a job in the works. We need a brave, reliable night watchman. And you can move up; we have a security team that you can join, once you can read and write and know some English.'

Brave! Reliable! Bhawar's chest swelled like a robin's. 'Sahib, the reading and writing and English are already as good as learned! I shall study every day, and watch all night, to be sure that your magnificent factory is as safe as . . . as the money-box of Ganesha!'

Worried, Urvashi interrupted the laughter. 'Then you don't think we should tell the police it was Bhawar who started it? Shouting Ram Ram?'

Bhawar deflated like a balloon. 'S-sahib . . . nahi, sahib!' he stammered. 'There were so many of them—I was afraid . . . afraid they'd take away the miss, I mean! And the men around were just standing . . . Something put it into my head . . . I wanted to wake them up, make them do something—'

'And you did it! And I'm very grateful, Bhawar!' With a twitch of a smile, Chandra reached out to touch her rescuer's hand. 'Don't blame him, uncle. He's not a fighting man, remember he told us? But he had to save me. It was a god put it into his mind.' And she knew which one. Could she tell them about Kali Mata? No; she could scarcely believe it herself.

'It was Ashish and his friend started it, not you, Bhawar,' Sita stated firmly. 'Urvashi, you want to get him arrested, sent to prison? Fine thanks that! Don't be silly.' She lifted an eyebrow at her husband.

He was smiling. 'Ji haa. I agree. I'm pleased to know that you're not a brainless thug, Bhawar, with nothing but a pair of fists. I'll remember it, when you're looking for promotion.' Everybody applauded.

Sita stood up, and waited till they were all looking at her before she spoke. She was more stern, more serious, than anyone could remember. 'But let this be a lesson to you, children. Never ever stir up religious trouble. Religious fanatics are like fireworks; start them off, and you can't stop them. Look at today. What did it say on the news? Fourteen in hospital, two serious, lucky no one killed? And all the damage, poor people's livelihoods ruined—all because of a wild shout. Remember it. Don't you stir it up—and don't be fools to be stirred up!'

Her husband looked at her quizzically. 'Ji haa, ji haa, maharishi, we hear and obey!' He bowed to her feet, and the mood lightened.

She wouldn't let it go so easily, though. 'My grandparents were all four murdered in the religious riots at the partition of India and Pakistan, at Independence. I don't want to lose any more of my family to other people's fanaticism. Or to their own! Now remember that, all of you!' She glared round. 'You get killed in a religious riot, and I'll . . . I'll never forgive you!'

Her husband chuckled. The children all laughed aloud. She glared, and then with a half-angry snort, she relaxed back to her normal cosy self. 'Ach, silly-billies! Vashi, your school uniform is dirtier than the maid's floor-cloth, and the laundry-man doesn't come till Thursday. Wash it in cold water first, to get the dye out, and then boil water and get it scrubbed and hung up on the roof right now. I'll iron it for you—you've still homework to do. Chandra's sari has four rips in it. I'll give it to the maid. Bhawar, my husband has another shirt for you, to replace that torn one.'

Delighted, Bhawar bowed his gratitude. Another hundred rupees at least from the old mem when he got home, a three-hundred-rupee shirt, a permanent job and promotion waiting for him! All for a few bumps, no worse than he'd had in the fields often, and the loss of his son's new shirt. He'd give another offering to Ganesha tonight; it obviously paid.

Chandra was apologizing. 'I'm sorry, Aunt Sita—'

'What have you to be sorry for, niece? You didn't do anything wrong!'

Chandra bit her lip. She had asked Durga for help—and got it. As Padma had warned her, the favour of the gods was dangerous.

CHAPTER 15

Goodbye

Ram Bhattacharjee was a huge man, whose high voice spoke in exclamation marks and who boasted with a jolly chuckle that he got more than his money's worth from airlines. 'Do I pay extra for overweight, like excess baggage-luggage? Nahi, nahi!' In his round, plump face, behind his round, plump glasses, his eyes were shrewd. He pressed a huge box of sweets tied with silver tinsel ribbons on Chandra. 'A gift for your aunt in England.'

'Oh, thank you, Mr Bhattacharjee—'

'Bapa!' he scolded her shrilly. 'You are my beti, remember!'

'Yes, bapa.' She was rather overwhelmed by his size, his fat laugh . . . her resentment at the thought of her lovely jewels . . . Oh, well.

Still and quiet between her grandmother and Urvashi in the back of his car, Chandra stewed gently in all her new warm clothes as they headed for Delhi International Airport in the cool just before dawn. Uncle Sunil was in the front seat beside Mr Bhattacharjee. Her case was in the boot, beside Mr Bhattacharjee's two huge cases; 'Tip-top quality woven silks and embroideries, samples to show the posh shops. Nothing but the best, the English say. And with you, I have two baggage allowances.' Bhawar was in there too, riding illegally with the boot lid open, but he'd not be left behind.

Mr Bhattacharjee had given her a walking stick. 'It is a quick-trick!' he beamed. 'If the nosy-poky immigration officers notice that you are two inches shorter than my Usha, they will be asking questions. So you will hop-step, and lean on the stick, and hide-slide past them! Accha?'

'Accha, Mr Bhattacharjee,' Chandra nodded. His glasses flashed. 'Bapa!'

He beamed, and nodded. 'Accha, beti!'

He had a very casual attitude to rules and regulations. Just as well, or she'd not be going with him . . . Oh, her lovely jewels! But now she'd be free of fear . . . She wished she felt less scared. But it was exciting, too.

When his creaky old car coughed and squeaked, Mr Bhattacharjee just laughed. 'It has flu, wheezing-sneezing, eh? Not what you expect from a rich international businessman! But nahi, I do not take taxi. A teeny-tiny little scam-scheme. I buy an old car—a banger, the English say—every time I go to England.' An early-rising cow suddenly wandered into the beam of the headlights. 'At least the brakes are strong! Sit back, please! I get it from a friend at a low-down price. And then I insure it, at a high-up rate! And I just leave it in the parking here, unlocked, and snip-snap it is stolen! Nahi, nahi, I don't arrange it, that would be dishonest! I make some poor man very happy, I give gifts, like Ganesha!' From the neck down, at least, he looked very like the fat elephant-headed god as he bubbled with laughter, his bulging belly wobbling against the wheel. 'So the insurance pays me the cost of a true-new car, and I pay no parking. Every little helps, the English say! Ah, here we are!'

Bhawar ran for a trolley for the luggage, and the huge man led them inside the airport hall. He looked at them all, and his grin faded. 'I'll go and check in our bags,' he said with surprising gentleness, and rolled off into the crowd.

Chandra clung to her grandmother's hand. 'Nani, England is so cold and dark, like winter all the time! I don't want to go! I'm scared!'

'And I don't want to lose you, either, child. But I'm old and tired, my dear.' True, under the fluorescent lights nani looked about four hundred years old, her eyes dull and sunken deep in their sockets. 'You must be brave, and go.

It won't be so very bad. Your aunt will be good to you. She'll love you like a mother.'

'Ha! Mata doesn't love me. Not as much as Padma did. Padma risked everything for me. Mata betrayed me. I hate her like a snake!'

Urvashi nodded, but nani tutted gently. 'Your poor mata! You mustn't think like that about her.'

'Why not?' Chandra felt bitterness boiling up in her. 'At least bapa didn't lie to me! But mata used to say the old ways were changing, and then she let me go, and she knew Roop was dead, she knew what would happen . . . How can she love me?' Tears flooded to her eyes. 'Oh, nani, I don't want to go away! Not again! Not alone! I'm scared!'

Helplessly, her grandmother hugged the girl. 'Hush, my dear!'

Sunil's face was grave. 'You're not alone, Chandra. You'll have your aunt, and you can write to Urvashi, and to your nani, and Sita.'

'And to Bhawar.' She smiled at him, where he stood in a light jacket and trouser suit, very proud of himself, but choked with emotion. 'I'll never forget you, Bhawar sahib, and all you did for me.'

'Miss . . . missy . . . I'll never . . . never . . . forget you either—I am all this because of you. You are a saint for me.' Bhawar gulped, and rubbed his eyes with his sleeve. 'You will send me a photo, please? To see what you are like in England?'

She nodded sideways. 'Of course. You'll have to practise your reading, and read my letters to your sons.'

'Ji haa. And miss—little brother—I have—' Shyly he offered her a small packet. 'A small nothing so that you will not forget us.'

'A gift? Ah, Bhawar, you are so good to me!' She didn't insult him by opening it. 'But I could never forget you anyway.'

'This is from Sangeeta,' Urvashi said, holding out a small packet. 'It's a pair of ear-rings, her own, to remind

111

you of her. She was so ashamed of what her father said. She loves you so much. And I put in a nose-stud, too. They are only silver, not gold, like your own, but—'

This proof of her friends' kindness and love was too much. Chandra started to sob in earnest. 'Hush, now!' nani urged her. 'Look, everyone's staring at us!'

'I don't care!' Chandra wailed. Urvashi's lips started to tremble in sympathy. Bhawar was sniffing.

'But I care!' They all jumped at the snap in the high voice. 'Behave yourself, both of you, all of you, and stop drawing attention! Look, the mem is upset, and so am I! Do you want her to fall sick? Or me to go off and leave you? Then be quite quiet!' Mr Bhattacharjee's jowls were trembling with anger. 'You're enough trouble to me. Double trouble, two of you weeping like a rain-drain! I'll not have it! You hear me? I'll not have it! Stop at once!'

Sunil had stiffened in annoyance at the scolding tone; out of the girls' sight, Mr Bhattacharjee gave him a wink. After a moment, Sunil relaxed. If it was a trick, it did seem to be working.

Chandra sniffed and struggled, and after a minute could dry her eyes, though her lips were still not quite under control. 'Accha! Much better!' Mr Bhattacharjee approved her. 'Crying babies never win the favour of the gods. Accha! For good girls, there is a nice-ice cream! Or a cool Pepsi, you would like, mem? And a small sip of beer for us men?' Sunil nodded thanks. Bhawar, in the background, muttered, 'An honour, sahib-ji!' Ram looked severe again. 'And then we go right away into Departure, and no more goodbyes and weeping-dripping!'

Under his determined eye, both Chandra and nani managed to stay calm, even when Urvashi burst into tears at parting. Nani even made herself smile. 'Remember, you aren't alone in your soul. I love you. And so do many other people. Sita, and Padma, and Sangeeta, and Bhawar, and Urvashi here.' Urvashi wailed agreement. Bhawar nodded, sniffing hard. The other men exchanged exasperated glances.

Nani swallowed bravely. 'And your mata—ji haa, I know you don't think so, but it is true. Even your bapa, in his own way. We all love you. We've done a lot for you. Don't let us down!' She hugged Chandra. 'Remember, this is the beginning of a new life for you. But don't forget us completely.'

'Nahi! Never, never, nani!'

'Come along, beti.' Mr Bhattacharjee patted Chandra's shoulder and tugged firmly. 'Goodbye, mem. Sahib. Miss.'

Chandra disengaged herself from nani's trembling arms. 'Goodbye, nani. I love you, too,' she whispered. 'Goodbye, Vashi. Goodbye and thank you, Bhawar. Goodbye, Uncle Sunil. Tell Aunt Sita I love her—I love you all. I'll not forget you, ever. I'll do my best.'

'Goodbye, Mr Bhattacharjee. Take care of yourself, granddaughter.' Nani sniffed, smiling valiantly. 'Chandra, I mean!' She waved, they all four waved, until Chandra had disappeared up the passage, and nani could let her emotions flow freely at last.

As they neared the Customs and Passport desk, Chandra cringed, but in fact the officials weren't worried by Mr Bhattacharjee or his 'daughter'. 'See her hair!' he complained jovially. 'Flu. Accha, flu! A temperature of a hundred and five, for four days, can you believe? So her nani cut her hair off to cool her! Old fashioned, eh? And eight kilos she lost! Eight kilos, in four days! And then yesterday she fell and hurt her foot. Elegant as a starving stork with three legs, eh? I don't want to take her, when she's such a fright-sight, but—' He heaved a shrug like a sea-elephant bull with hiccups. 'Her mata insisted. She bullies me. Nahi, truly, don't laugh! I shiver-quiver at the sound of her voice! Ganesha be kind to us poor husbands!'

Laughing with him, swamped by the flood of words, they stamped his passport and papers, almost ignoring Chandra cowering and clinging to his arm under all their eyes. She tried not to show her relief; she was through the first barrier.

Uncle Sunil had said the long flight would be boring; Chandra found it very interesting. Ram Bhattacharjee squeezed into his seat; 'Sardines would go on strike!' What did he mean? It was much roomier than the bus to Jaisalmer. She clutched his hand through the high whine and thrust of take-off, and paid anxious attention to the stewardesses' talk about life-jackets and emergency exits. No one had ever suggested to Chandra that she might feel sick, so she didn't, though her ears popped rather painfully. That frightened her till her 'bapa' told her to swallow to cure it; she sat swallowing diligently for nearly five minutes after they'd levelled off, until her mouth was quite dry.

After a while, she remembered and opened the little parcel from Bhawar. It was, as she had half expected, a tiny silvery figure of Ganesha, to open her path and make a good beginning for her in this terrifying new world. She would write and thank Bhawar—nani would read him the letter, or his son's teacher. Almost in tears again, she tucked the charm away safely in her purse. Ganesha was god of money, too; he would be happy there.

There were so many white people! Even the servants—stewardesses—they were white, too. She didn't dare ask for anything. She enjoyed the meals, though they needed lots more spice. However, once Mr Bhattacharjee confidently called the stewardess to show her how to work the headphones, the in-flight film helped her relax. And when it was finished, and the news, there was music, of four different kinds. And a magazine to read, free . . . Tired out, after six hours she fell asleep to the strains of Mantovani and didn't wake till the stewardess bent over her to strap her in for landing at Manchester.

The bright sky vanished, and the plane was enveloped in white clouds. In the semi-dark, Chandra's stomach tensed rigid with fear. Durga, Ganesha, all gods help her . . . She tried to tell herself it was just because of the pressure in her ears, the anxiety of landing, but it wasn't. She was so scared . . . If they caught her, what would they do? Send her back to bapa, or even to Rajasthan? She couldn't bear it . . .

When the plane bumped on to the runway, she yelped in sheer fright.

By the time Chandra had to face officials for the second time, in the crush of the Foreign Nationals' queue, she was on the point of fainting. Even Mr Bhattacharjee was sweating gently, in spite of the cold. If he was scared too—quick, try to think of something else. Aunt Sita had been quite right, it really was chilling-freezing. Could it be like this all year? And it was so dark, she could see through the window, so grey and miserable . . . Oh, please let her get through! Please . . .

The Indian official at the Immigration desk eyed Chandra shrewdly. Half paralysed by panic, like a frog by a snake, she tried not to show it, not to shudder or collapse, not to stare blindly, not to grin, to look round as if she was relaxed and interested, not terrified . . .

After a century, the woman sniffed, nodded and stamped the documents. Mr Bhattacharjee winked in vast relief to Chandra as they were passed through. She was in . . .

They collected their luggage from the carousel—a magic thing, but Chandra had no spirit to relish it. Customs—no, nothing to declare. As Mr Bhatacharjee surged happily along the final corridor, Chandra tried to believe it. She was in, really in, past the officials. Slowly, excitement was rising in her, displacing the terrible anxiety, the strain, the tiredness . . . She was in England! She was safe, free, free!

Beyond the door into the main hall, behind a waist-high barrier, crowds of people were waiting and waving, brown and white faces smiling or anxious. Chandra peered

115

forward, but they were a blur . . . Where was Mr
Bhattacharjee? Chandra turned back. He had gone—in
the crowd, he had vanished. Her heart stopped.

She was alone. She was twelve years old, and she was
alone. She had lost her parents, her brothers, her friends
and teachers at school; Padma, Bhawar; nani; Urvashi and
the rest of the Mukherjee family. Everyone who knew her
and cared for her was gone, even Mr Bhattacharjee. She
was alone, in a strange country, among strange people . . .
she would die of loneliness . . . Oh, Durga . . .

A trolley stopped by her side, and her escort was there
again. He was smiling fatly, like a huge version of a little
Chinese brass god nani had in one of her display cases. She
started to breathe again, with a gasp of relief that made him
chuckle.

'You will quick-soon see your aunt. Accha. I think we are
finished now, all done as agreed? No hanky-panky, all
satisfied customers, no returned seconds? Accha, OK.' He
patted Chandra's cheek with a pudgy finger. 'You're a good
girl. I thought at first maybe you were bad, flighty-naughty,
and that was why your relations were sending you so far
away. But no. You're a good girl, in a bad situation. It is a
pity you could not stay in India, but—' he studied her
again. 'But maybe not. Here you have a fresh start. It will
be difficult, but at least far from your in-laws. May all the
gods help you, and bless you with success and happiness.'
He held out his hand. Trying to smile, Chandra laid her
own small fingers in his huge, gentle fist.

'You go on now, meet your aunt. I will wait, I promise,
till I see you with her. But you don't turn round, don't
introduce us. You forget me, OK? If you get into trouble
after, don't involve me, I don't know you! Accha? Best of
luck!' Solemnly, then with a wide smile, he shook her hand.
'Best luck!' he repeated in English, handed her her small
case and the box of sweets, and waved her ahead of him.

Hesitantly, Chandra walked forward into the enor-
mously high, echoing hall. Suddenly one figure behind

the rail sprang sharp into focus. There—a small lady in a blue coat over a green sari, the image of mata's wedding photograph, it must be Aunt Manju. The lady's eyes passed right over her niece, and then swung back. 'Chandra? Chandra! You remember me? Oh, you're so tall, and so like your father!' she called in English, reaching to take the girl's hands.

'Aunt Manju? Oh, Aunt Manju!' With no warning, Chandra's knees nearly melted. They leaned over the barrier to hug each other.

A huge form lumbered past them, with a fat, satisfied chuckle, and disappeared into the crowd.

'I'm so glad to see you! You'll be quite safe here, my dear,' Manju was murmuring confidently. 'All your troubles are over.'

For a moment, Chandra quailed. It was tempting the gods, to say such a thing! She'd like to believe it, but . . .

Her heart swelled. She hugged Aunt Manju back, with a suddenly joyful strength. She was alive, and free, with a new family and a new life in front of her. She'd make more friends. The world did change. She would believe it. Even if all her troubles weren't over, she'd manage.

She was Chandra!

GLOSSARY

accha: exclamation; good, fine, well done!
bapa: father.
beti: daughter.
brahmin: priest; member of highest caste.
caste: rigid system of class separation.
chai: tea.
chapatti: pancake-like bread.
charpoy: bedframe of wood with string lacing to hold sleeping mat.
coolie: street cleaner, bearer.
dowry: money or gifts (e.g. scooter, fridge) from parents of bride, given to or often demanded by parents of groom; officially illegal.
dupatta: women's scarf, part of salwar suit, draped across chest or shoulder.
ekka: small pony carriage.
Eve-teasers: youths who try to embarrass girls.
ghee: butter, boiled and allowed to set to help it keep better.
-ji: honorific; added to a person's name or title, to show respect.
ji haa: yes.
jungly: bad-mannered, ignorant person, oaf.
kameez: tunic top, down to knees, of women's suit.
lakh: any huge number.
louchi: kind of feather-light bun.
lunghi: waist-cloth, a cross between a loin-cloth and a sarong.
Mahabharata: Hindu epic story.
maharajah, maharani: great king, queen.
maharishi: great religious teacher.

mata: mother.

mem: memsahib, lady.

nahi: no.

namaste, namaskar: greeting; hello, good day, etc.

nani: grandmother.

paisa: penny; four paise = one rupee.

pan: mixture of betel nuts, leaves, and lime, faintly intoxicating and relaxing; people chew it and spit out the red juice.

pooja: worship, prayers.

purdah: custom of keeping women strictly away from men of other families.

puri: small, round cake of unleavened wheat flour, deep fried in ghee or oil.

Rajput: noble, especially in Rajasthan; member of high caste.

rupee: coin. £1 = approximately 45 rupees, at time of writing.

sahib: sir, boss, gentleman.

salwar: trousers of women's suit.

samosa: pastry folded and cooked round filling of meat or vegetables.

sati: old custom of widow burning herself with husband's body; now illegal.

swastika: lucky wheel pattern, a cross with each arm bent at right angles, symbolizing peace.

tilak: cosmetic mark between eyebrows.

zemindar: landowner, squire.

The Hindu religion says that all gods, Hindu or other, are different facets of the one basic GOD, the essential spirit of the universe, described as Brahman. Creation, Preservation, and Destruction are represented by the trinity formed by Brahma, Shiva, and Vishnu. Most Hindus follow either Shiva or Vishnu who have various forms, male and female, with different powers and interests. Worshippers choose which form to pray to depending on what they want.

Rama and Krishna are perhaps the most popular incarnations of Vishnu. In the Mahabharata, Krishna states, 'Whichever God you pray to, it is I who answer.'